A Wisp of F

The Story of Ailean "Nan Sop" Maclean

Scotland's Last Viking Pirate

Historical Fiction

by David Nash

Collins Publishing

Vincit Pericula Virtus

O'Coileain

Vincit Pericula Virtus

1st Edition
ISBN-13: 9781700276926

Foreword by Ronald W. Collins

David Nash has done a remarkable job of putting perspective on the many myths and historical facts concerning Allen "Nan Sop" Maclean. Creating a reasonable and convincing story from a small handful of historical facts is a daunting task. Nash has accomplished that with this book. He had to tackle the many conflicting sources, separate myth from fact and then weave it all into a story that puts flesh onto the bare bones we know about Nan Sop.

Even answering the simple question of how long did Allen Nan Sop live? We have four main historical sources: the 1838, An Historical and Genealogical Account of the Clan Maclean by a Seneachie; the 1889, A History of the Clan MacLean by J.P. MacLean; the 1899, The Clan Gillean by A. Maclean Sinclair and the 1995, Warriors and Priests by Nicholas Maclean-Bristol. Maclean-Bristol is by far the most accurate and well researched. All four rely on earlier works and sources.

So, when did Nan Sop live? The Seneachie states without mentioning the year that Nan Sop "died at an advanced age." He goes on later to say the "Earl of

Lennox, in his treasonable alliance with the King of England, during the regency of the Earl of Arran and in the minority of Queen Mary, succeeded in attaching the warlike Allen to his interest. He accompanied the Earl on a certain mission to England in the character of ambassador from the self-styled Lord of the Isles, James Macdonald of Isla. For this and other treasonable practices he, however succeeded sometime after in obtaining a pardon from Queen Mary." Seneachie, pg 41.

Seneachie does not say he met with Mary Queen of Scots, only that he received a pardon from her. Nan Sop went to England during the time when Lennox was in alliance with a "King of England". That King had to be Henry VIII who reigned until 1547. So, Nan Sop probably was in England before 1547.

J.P. MacLean simply states that "Allan died in 1551, in bed." pg. 89

A. Maclean Sinclair says that, "In July, 1539, Ailein nan Sop received from the Government a gift of the non-entry mails of Gigha and certain lands in Kintyre and Islay. In 1552, Hector, his son and successor, received a gift of the same lands. In 1554, Neil Macneill, who had unquestionably a better right to Gigha than

Hector Mac Allan, sold his claim to James Macdonald of Islay. Hector Mac Allan, who was in possession of Gigha, refused to part with it." pg. 104. If Hector inherited his father's lands in 1552 then Nan Sop died in late 1551 or early 1552.

Sinclair later states that, "Allan died at peace with his church, on his bed in Tarbert Castle, in the year 1551, and was buried with his ancestors on the sacred Isle of Iona. He was probably about fifty-three years of age." pg. 426 Meaning he was born in 1498 and died in 1551.

Nicholas Maclean-Bristol in "Warriors and Priests" says on page 76 that Lachlan Cattanach's two sons "were evidently of age in 1520s, they were probably born in the 1490s." Later, on page 130, he states "Sometime after 1551 when he... lost a staunch supporter by the death of Ailean nan sop." "Allan was dead by January 1551/2 when his son Hector received a grant of the 20 pound lands of Gigha."

The timing around Mary, Queen of Scots, is really jumbled in the three 19th century MacLean sources. Mary, Queen of Scots ascended the throne in 1542, she reigned over Scotland from 14 December 1542 to 24 July 1567, so there was no visit in 1532 as stated in one source. Mary was

5

the only surviving legitimate child of King James V of Scotland, and was only <u>six days old in 1542 when James died</u>. She spent most of her childhood in France while Scotland was ruled by regents, and in 1558, she married the Dauphin of France, Francis. Mary was queen consort of France from his accession in 1559 until his death in December 1560. Widowed, Mary returned to Scotland, arriving in Leith on 19 August 1561, ten years after Allen Nan Sop died. Four years later, she married her half-cousin, Henry Stuart, Lord Darnley, and in June 1566 they had a son, James. If Nan Sop received a pardon from her, then it was probably not in person.

Henry VIII was King of England until 1547 and then his son Edward VI ruled from 1547 until 1553. Then Henry's daughter Mary, Bloody Mary, was Queen. Mary I was the Queen of England and Ireland from July 1553 until her death in 1558. She is best known for her aggressive attempt to reverse the English Reformation, which had begun during the reign of her father, Henry VIII. So, if Allen visited Queen Mary it means he lived until after 1553.

How to make sense of all this??

Reaching an age of 53 was not considered an advanced age, even in the

16th century. The dates of when Mary Queen of Scots and Bloody Mary reigned are well documented. Mary of Scots is very unlikely to have met with Nan Sop. She would have been 9 years old when Nan Sop died. Could her regents, in her name, have issued Nan Sop a pardon? It's possible because they were trying to strengthen Scotland's claim to independence from England and having Nan Sop on their side (or at least not on England's side) would have been a good thing. So, he could have been pardoned by Mary in her minority as a result of regents.

The trip to England most likely involved Henry VIII and not Bloody Mary so it could have been any time before 1547. That fits with a death date for Nan Sop of 1551.

So, the question comes down to when exactly did Hector, son of Nan Sop, inherit his father's lands? I trust Maclean-Bristol's research when he says he inherited in 1552. Therefore, I conclude Nan Sop died in late 1551 or early 1552. Therefore, he never met Bloody Mary. If he received a pardon from Mary of Queen Scots, it was not in person.

Nash also had to sort through the many myths involving Allen Nan Sop. Those he chose to weave into this book are those that meet the reasonable test as based upon historic fact, at least partially.

David Nash captures the animosity between the Clan MacLean and the Clan Campbell and their Chief, the Earl of Argyll better than any history book.

The author has used the archaic spellings of names for both Ailean (Allen) and his brother Eachann (Hector Mor), and others, such as Tearlach (Charles) and as much setting texture, i.e. details of weapons, clothing, towns, ships, etc., as he could to put the reader into the time of Nan Sop.

It has been my pleasure to be David Nash's historical consultant for this project and I applaud him for staying true to what history we know of Allen "Nan Sop" MacLean.

Ronald W. Collins, author of
The Genealogy of the Clan MacLean

Dedication

This book could not have been written without the dedicated research of Ronald Collins, a genealogist and Historian for Clan MacLean.

While I have used other sources for this work to provide color and background, His definitive series on the MacLean Clan has provided the historical basis for the novel.

As with most of my books, there needs to be an acknowledgment of the places and people who put up with me while I wrote it.

Thanks to the owners of Coppertoppe Inn and Retreat Center in New Hampshire, a haven for writers who need that quiet place to think, write, and edit those last few chapters. Great food, a wonderfully peaceful atmosphere, and a terrific view!

Thanks to my waitresses and the wonderful owner, Cassie, at Mae's Cafe in Wickford, Rhode Island where I spent many a caffeine filled afternoon struggling to get the flow and pacing for this novel. The food is delicious, and I would certainly gain twenty pounds there if it wasn't for my trainer and dance partners!

And finally, to Mauna Loa Kea (2007-2019), my 'little supervisor' Maltese for the past ten years, who kept me from aches and pains by climbing across me every twenty minutes for a better sleeping position and demanding that I take her out and get some exercise myself. I would surely be a grouchy crippled old man now without your love and encouragement to, "get out and do!" and not just write. You will be sorely missed.

Contents

List of Images

Maps

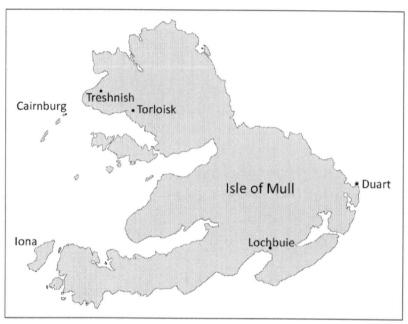

Map 1 - Isle of Mull

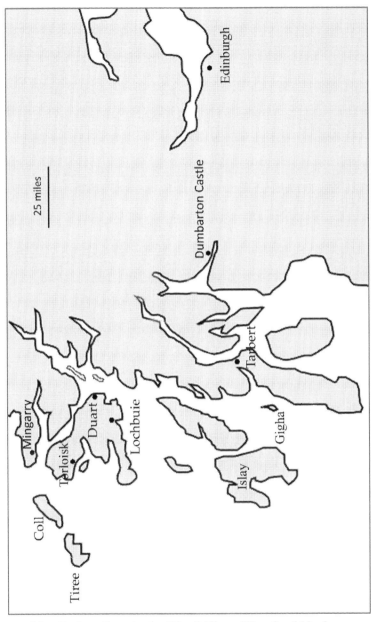

Map 2 - Locations in the life of Ailean "Nan Sop" MacLean

25 miles

Edinburgh

Dumbarton Castle

Tarbert

Mingarry

Torloisk

Duart

Lochbuie

Gigha

Islay

Coll

Tiree

Chapter One

The Dreams of Cairnburg

Ailean was falling.

Wind rushed by his ears. He was going to die. He heard a harsh bellow and the sound of waves crashing into the rocks below.

Then he stopped. He was hovering, floating serenely above the waves below the edge of the cliff. Breathing was difficult.

He looked up the shear face of a stone cliff. Looming above him, he could see the face of a man looking down like some angered ancient god.

He was short but broad shouldered with a thick beard and dark red hair. The man's face grew larger as he spoke swimming in Ailean's vision. He changed from a stranger to his father, then his mother, then back to himself again. All the faces were enraged. Angry and anxious and disappointed. His own cheeks grew red looking at those faces.

"And that's the last chance you'll ever get to disgrace a Lady!" boomed the voice of the stranger.

"The last chance...," echoed in his head.

Beside the man, he could see the form of his beloved, a dark shadow outlined in sunlight. There was a halo, a golden nimbus of light surrounding her. It floated around her golden hair. However, she hesitated, avoiding the edge, and refusing to look down.

"Is... is he dead?"

Her voice was soft and carried out on the wind. It echoed off the angled walls of the cliff. The voice changed with each echo. First, it seemed melancholy, then expectant, then strangely cruel. A bird screamed in the distance. He looked into a cloudy, darkening sky, but could not see it.

"Nah, the lucky sod landed on a ledge. He can stay there and rot. The sides are sheer and the earth crumbles to touch. He won't be climbing out. And he'll not be harming any more women after this. We'll leave him and head back to the castle. The Chief will probably make us haul him up for beheading after a while."

"I don't think so," said her soft voice.

"Now," he thought. "Now, she will speak and clear my name. Now, she'll explain it's a misunderstanding. Now, she will tell him of her feelings for me."

His mind drifted to a perfumed note in his pocket. The promise it held.

Instead, a harsh voice grated above him.

"Why not? He chased you out of the castle onto the moor. I heard you screaming that you are for God. But it sure wasn't praying he had in mind. I mean, beheading is too good for him, and I'd like to see him just left there for the birds to pick at."

He sniffed.

"The Chief will make an example, though."

Her voice trembled.

He knew what was coming. Not the salvation he hoped for. Once again, he felt the earth slide beneath him. The high shear walls of the cliff grew larger, and the people got smaller, more distant.

Her voice twisted, becoming the harsh cry of an angry bird of prey. Then came the words he did not want to hear.

"I think not. You see, that's his son down there..."

* * *

And suddenly he was standing on the small shelf of rock, humbling himself before a man who demanded he abandon his love, seek no further contact, seek no reprisal against him or his family. He demanded, and despite his pride, he yielded and promised.

And she stood high above him and said not a word while his dreams crashed — leaving nothing but a dark emptiness.

* * *

He surged awake, his body covered in sweat despite the dampness of the stone and straw of his bedding.

His last thought before full wakefulness was a shout.

"That's not the way it happened!"

Photo 1 - The ruins of Cairnburg Castle

Chapter Two

Schemes and Machinations

Striding away down the hallway, Eachann MacLean could not believe what he just heard. His father, Lachlan, was planning to give away part of his inheritance to his brother!

"I am the first born male! I am the heir! What could my father be thinking to give away lands I should rightfully rule!"

He stalked the cold stone walls of Duart castle fuming. The castle was damp and the light from smoky torches was the only illumination. He turned a corner and almost blundered into Tearlach MacLean.

Tearlach jumped back.

"Pardon, cousin," he said. "I did not

see you coming around the corner."

Tearlach was tall and rangy, with a solid upper body from years of hunting in the highlands. Long black hair was disheveled, and a fierce beard complemented his hawk-like face.

"At least the man is honest, even if he does fawn over my little brother."

Although annoyed, Eachann donned a forgiving face.

"My fault as well, cousin. Let us think no more of it."

Tearlach grinned.

"Pity you weren't Lady Anne. There's a collision I could appreciate!"

Eachann put on a conspiratorial smile.

Lady Anne was a Treshnish MacLean who had come to visit in the summer. She was slender and graceful, with long jet-black hair, brown eyes, and a tom-boyishness that appealed to the clearly smitten Tearlach.

"Fancy her, do you? Well, I can't fault your taste."

Tearlach caught himself and looked chagrined. Then he brightened.

"I'm off to the axe toss in town! Hugh the blacksmith is hosting it to show off the balance of his newest work."

Eachann was instantly bored, but he did not show it. It wouldn't do for the future Chief to appear disinterested.

He nodded and gestured for Tearlach to pass by.

"Well then," he said. "Best of luck! What's the prize?"

"A repaired hauberk from an English foot soldier."

Eachann nodded.

"English? A fine prize. I wonder how Hugh came by it."

Tearlach looked thoughtful.

"Don't have the faintest idea. But I know I would like to win it."

"Well you better hurry to the field if you want a chance."

Tearlach waved and dashed off.

Eachann ran his fingers through his long brown hair.

He would need to speed up his plans if he was going to preserve his future estate.

England wouldn't be far enough for his brother to go, he decided.

"Hell might be a good choice though."

* * *

Lachlan MacLean had a serious problem. Since the incident at Cairnburg castle with Ailean and the daughter of MacNeil of Barra, his wife had been pressuring him to give his younger son some responsibility.

"He's a good boy," his wife proclaimed. "He just did something foolish, egged on by alcohol and those damn friends of his!"

"Perhaps," he replied, "But it lost me a valuable alliance and a good trading partner, at least for a while."

"Well," she replied. "With lands and a title, he'd have to buckle down, wouldn't he?"

She touched his hand gently. "He hasn't been the same since you brought us back to Duart."

Lachlan's hand clenched slightly at the mention of his hasty return from Cairnburg.

He had to admit she had a point. Deciding what lands to give the lad was the real problem. After some discussion with his advisers he thought he finally had a solution.

Lachlan smiled at his wife.

"Ailean will become Chieftain of the new estate of Killundine in Morvern. There's already a small castle with a good view of the waterway and a small protected inlet for sheltering ships."

Lachlan thought it was a good choice.
"The lad loves the ocean. He'll probably spend more time on a ship than governing his lands."

He shook his head thinking about Ailean's growing surliness toward life.

"His 'indiscretion' just seemed to take on a life of its own. They even named the damned shelf he landed on after him. No wonder he's so bitter."

He sighed and turned to his wife.

"We'll award him his title at the end of the week when there are credible witnesses who will help him administer his lands."

She leaned over and gave him a peck on the cheek.

"He'll surprise you. I'm sure of it."

"Oh Lord," thought Lachlan, *"I hope not."*

* * *

Ailean slipped into the barrack. Despite his MacLean bearing, broad shoulders, and muscular arms, no one paid particular attention to his arrival - as he hoped. His long reddish gold hair drew no notice among the sailors. Many of them had Norse blood as well. Clansmen were interested in their drinks — not the comings and goings of others.

The smell in the barrack was a mixture of ale, sweat, and wet straw. Ailean did not find it offensive, though he preferred the smell of the open sea.

He had been coming to this place for several weeks now during odd hours. He marked the men who were regulars, and those who seemed to be new. He watched to see who was respected and who was not. He gauged the men's strength and watched how they walked. His casual glance could identify a man back from the sea. Their gait was strange as if they expected the floor to move under them.

There were a few fights. Places like this always had a few. His slate gray eyes watched these carefully. He watched to see who stood up and who backed down. He watched to see who had friends and who did not.

But his time of watching was done. He brushed back a lock of unruly hair and stroked a neatly trimmed beard. He touched a small purse at his side.

It was time to act...

Photo 2 - Duart Castle

Chapter Three

Shaming

"Banquet meals are never a pleasant time for Ailean," Tearlach thought.

They sat in a large hall filled with lively chatter, none of it directed at them. No one wanted to be seen talking to Ailean, lest some of the stain on his reputation rubbed off on them.

Tearlach made it a point to sit with Ailean, whenever decorum permitted. Affairs of state sometimes barred him from sitting with his cousin, but for most meals they sat together, sometimes discussing local affairs and local gossip, but often simply eating as companions.

Lately the silence seemed more

pronounced to Tearlach, as if there was a storm brewing and directed at them.

To his credit, Ailean bore the silence with a stoic resolution. He had little to fear in his father's castle, except the occasional smirk or jibe said just a bit too loudly.

Today was a special day.

Several important persons had arrived recently at the castle and Ailean was seated with his father and brothers, Eachann and Patrick, at the head table.

Ailean's mother was not in attendance, claiming to have come down with a chill. She was resting in her rooms while attendants fussed over her.

Tearlach smiled at the thought of the feisty women surrounded by a horde of women offering various bad tasting remedies, while she tried to fend them off long enough to get some sleep.

"I bet she has a couple of them wishing they could flee to another castle after two more days."

Tearlach understood that Lady Marian was always sick whenever Patrick was in attendance at an event. She wanted nothing to do with the bastard her husband had sired. Tearlach was certain that if she were not a Christian, she would have poisoned the child and his mother by now.

32

Ailean sat near the end of one of the tables, his older brother sat next to his father. Patrick, the youngest was a scrawny lad, unlike his older brothers. However, he sat dutifully between them and tried to follow conversations while drawing as little attention to himself as possible. This was fairly easy with Ailean around to draw the majority of interest and ire.

The tables had been laid out in a "U" shape in the great hall. The family members sat at the arch with Lachlan in the center. Eachann sat to his right and Patrick to his immediate left. Ailean sat to the left of Patrick. Tables extended down to accommodate the visiting guests, but Tearlach noticed that for some reason the guests were lined up to the right of Chief Lachlan and most of the people who were friends and supporters of Eachann were position to the left on the same side as Ailean.

"This is not good," he thought. But there was nothing he could do about it.

There were no weapons allowed at the meal, save the knives used to cut meat.

Tearlach braced himself for a long meal.

A serving girl, Fiona, brought him a large piece of roasted boar, which he began to chew with great relish. She smiled and for a moment his thoughts drifted to a more pleasant way to spend the evening. She seemed to sense his thoughts. Fiona smiled and turned, walking away with a sway to her hips that was not there earlier.

Tearlach grinned.

She had long red hair that moved like waves as she walked and sea green eyes. He wondered if her mother had been a prize in an Irish raid.

It was then that he heard the comment.

"Perhaps it is the only way he can get a woman?" said a voice further up the table.

"Certainly, it cannot be! He only falls for those who run away!" came the laughing reply.

A few others joined in the laughter.

Tearlach noticed that the voices had been pitched so only those near the corner could hear it. Tearlach's hearing was exceptional from years spent hunting in the forests. He could lock in on a sound and follow it. He realized that Ailean's face was turning red. It was clearly an insult directed at him, but both Tearlach and Ailean knew that if he said anything, they would have some feeble excuse for why it was spoken of someone else.

Ailean did not take the bait. Though he clearly heard what was said, he made no move and uttered no sound.

A blonde-haired serving girl who was standing near him stepped back. Ailean winced but remained silent. Then he did something that Tearlach had never seen him do. His face relaxed. There was a hint of a smile, a joke shared among friends, and he looked at each of the laughing men in turn.

Tearlach was struck with an unreasoning fear.

The face was smiling, but the eyes were utterly cold. And as Ailean's eyes made contact with each person at the table, the laughter died, and they looked away.

Slowly the laughter ceased. One man instinctively reached for a weapon that was not at his side.

Ailean said nothing. He just looked at each man in turn.

"Marking them in his mind, committing their faces to memory," Tearlach thought.

Tearlach knew at that moment with utter certainty that each of them was a dead man.

The lack of conversation at a large section of the table drew the attention of

Lachlan who leaned forward and looked down the length of the table. Lachlan was a formidable fighter and time had not dulled his instincts. His bushy eyebrows furrowed, and he licked his thick lips.

"Is there some issue?" He asked in a slow, rumbling voice.

Eachann's voice was calm and smooth.

"Probably just the coincidence of each man taking a bite at the same time, father."

Eachann was smiling with a great show of perfect white teeth. His face was relaxed and calm. His eyes were like his mother's, a dark green that reminded one more of moss than of emeralds.

If Lachlan noticed that no one was chewing he kept the fact to himself.

Ailean rose from the table slowly. He seemed to sway a bit as he stood.

He was of above average height, but his large shoulders and muscular arms made him look even larger. He had a solid frame that showed no signs of softness.

"Excuse me. I fear I must go."

Lachlan smiled.

"A bit too much? That I understand. Go."

Tearlach wondered if Lachlan did actually understand. It was uncharacteristic of him to let anyone leave from the head table so quickly.

Ailean swayed a bit more and then made his way down the back of the table. Eyes watched him warily as he passed each of his tormentors in turn. However, he did nothing. Reaching the end of the table, he turned and made his way out the door heading in the direction of fresh air.

It was a good act, but Tearlach was not fooled. He had seen Ailean drink far more than he had consumed tonight and bury an axe dead center in the target on a wager.

Tearlach was curious however, at Ailean's choice of words as he weaved slightly walking down the aisle. All he said was, "Never again."

Chapter Four

Away in the Night

"Where the hell did Ailean go?" Tearlach wondered for the thirteenth time as he scoured the alleys and byways looking for his friend.

Duart castle was a large structure and the town that had sprung up at its base was growing as more people came seeking the stability and steady work offered by one of the larger clans in Scotland. People did not move much, but the influx was steady, and the town was growing.

Unlike many people who would make for a woman to assuage his troubles, Ailean liked to head off to wander the streets of the small village outside the castle and brood.

There was, of course, trouble to be found in drunken fools, but Ailean looked forward to it. He savored a good fight and he had emerged from more than one encounter with a knife cut or a bruise from a narrowly avoided blade or truncheon.

Tearlach had long ago stopped worrying for his friend when he went off on these forays. In fact, most of the clansmen had learned to vanish when Ailean's form prowled the walkways.

Tearlach was more careful, checking both the sides and the rooftops before venturing in. He also brought a distant cousin with him for support. Trouble was a lot less likely to attack two people, especially when they were in MacLean tutelage and carrying weapons as he and Brodie were doing now. Still, he usually went only a few paces into a shadowed entrance, enough to assure himself that Ailean was not there, then backed out and tried another.

He had covered all the major routes his friend normally followed and had finally turned to the docks as a last resort. Ailean loved the sea, but his walks rarely took him there. It was a frustration that he could not go to sea. His mother had been instrumental in barring ocean adventures, limiting his early excursions to the local harbor. Lately, however, Tearlach had heard that Ailean had been seen at a barrack near the docks. It was a good place to let off steam as long as no one reached for a dirk.

As Tearlach and Brodie were making their way out onto one of the docks running parallel to the shoreline, he heard a thump and a short cry.

He looked over at Brodie. Brodie had crouched down a bit and looked back. Both nodded and made their way towards the sound.

A group of men were hastily readying Laird Lachlan's favorite ship for sea. Supplies were being carried on board. The soft cry was from a man whose foot was obviously just under a box that had fallen over.

He was hopping around and muttering soft curses under his breath.

In the center of all this activity was Ailean.

"Ailean, what are you doing?" called Tearlach.

"Quiet, fool!" came a hissing reply. "What does it look like I'm doing? I'm leaving this godforsaken pile of dung and heading to sea!"

"What? Are you out of your mind! In your father's ship?"

"He doesn't need it. He's got dozens more."

Ailean looked around.

"Besides this one's pretty. Has good lines. Will make a fine ship for going a Viking..."

Ailean swayed slightly as he said this.

"He is drunk!" thought Tearlach. *"But he's obviously been planning this for a long time. Otherwise he wouldn't have a crew."*

Tearlach looked at the men who were gazing about warily now, looking for guards or others who might be coming.

"We're coming aboard, Ailean."

He added for the men surrounding him.

"And we're alone."

The men relaxed the barest bit. Ailean seemed to sense the mood through his alcoholic fog.

"They are all right. Back to work."

Men jumped back to loading the ship with provisions. They were stocking for a long voyage.

He approached Ailean warily. It was best not to anger him when he was in one of his moods. He could act unpredictably, even with friends.

"So, you weren't going to invite me?" he said in a low voice when they were closer.

"Didn't think you would come. And you would have wasted a lot of my time trying to talk me out of it."

"True," said Tearlach. Tearlach looked around at all the activity.

"But it looks like you've thought this through, and you will be leaving soon..."

"Tonight. As soon as the ship is loaded."

"Where are the guards? Did you hurt them?"

"A few are loading the ship; others are on a long patrol on the far side. There will be an incident that will keep them there for a while."

Ailean shrugged.

"A bit of bribery for a couple of agents, a staged incident to keep the rest occupied. The men loading are joining me."

"And where did you get the rest of this crew?"

"Been recruiting carefully down at the docks for several weeks now. I have money, and I have a name..." He paused as if a bad taste were in his mouth. "Even if it is infamous."

He smiled without any trace of mirth.

"Among the people I wanted, my reputation is almost a badge of honor."

Now that Tearlach was closer, he could smell the alcohol on Ailean's breath.

"What about your father? He'll be furious." He may even have you hunted down."

"No, he won't! He'll be happy to get rid of me! He can distance his reputation from mine and repair some of the alliances I... damaged."

"Besides," his voice became heavier, more menacing. "I have some scores to settle that being the second son of Lachlan Maclean prevents. As the Laird of Duart and Chief of all the Maclean Clan, he can't abide such actions."

Tearlach thought back to the table and the look he gave to the men at it.

"Yes," he thought *"Ailean has some scores he wants to settle. And he can't do it if he is sitting at his father's table."*

Suddenly he knew what he must do.

"I'm coming with you," he announced. He heard Brodie's sharp intake of breath.

"Brodie will stay and help cover our tracks until we are out of the harbor and gone..."

Brodie gave him a quizzical look.

Tearlach returned his gaze and gave a

small wink that no one else could see.

Ailean's jaw opened and closed silently.

Tearlach rushed on before Ailean could object.

"People know I left looking for you. There is no way they would believe I wasn't helping you leave. If I stay, I'm for the dungeons, sure."

He looked at Ailean.

"You know it's true."

He took a breath and rushed on.

"If I go, I'll get adventure, and you will get someone who will watch your back."

Tearlach looked meaningfully around the ship. These men were not to be trusted; they were not MacLeans.

"What about Brodie? What of his fortunes? He won't be so pretty looking after a month in the dungeon, either."

He heard a man next to Ailean bark a short laugh. Ailean looked over and the man made himself scarce.

Tearlach continued.

"Brodie will say we didn't find you. We were seen looking for you together. Then we split up. He went to the battlements and I went to the docks to cover more ground. Both have guards so we were in little danger of attack. He didn't know it was a trick and I was going with you."

Tearlach smiled.

Lachlan will be suspicious, but he won't do anything. Brodie's from a good family."

Ailean looked thoughtful.

"It won't be an easy ride, Tearlach."

Tearlach laughed.

"It never is with you, Ailean."

"You will follow my orders, no matter what they are."

For just a moment, Tearlach hesitated. There was a coldness in Ailean's eyes now that no amount of alcohol could hide. A determination and a raw anger that would brook no challenge. You would obey Ailean, or you would die.

Tearlach almost stopped then, but he knew he was already past the point of return.

"Understood, captain."

"Good," said Ailean. "Get Brodie ashore. He can cut over to the battlements from the north and none will be the wiser as to how much time he spent searching before getting there."

"Tearlach walked Brodie to the end of the dock."

His voice became a whisper.

45

"Follow the route Ailean gave you. But when you reach the headland to the west head back to the castle. Tell Chief Lachlan that Ailean is very drunk and has taken a ship to avoid a fight with allies who have given him a mortal insult. When he is sober, and they have left, he will return."

Brodie looked surprised.

"After a few weeks at sea, this lot may be more interested in dry land than waves, and I can persuade Ailean to reconcile with Chief Lachlan. The Chief, will decide the right of it when I have told him of the insult offered which I overheard. It will be his decision, of course, but I expect he will think a two or three week borrowing of a birlinn a small price for avoiding losing alliances."

Brodie nodded.

"Good luck, Tearlach. You are a true friend. I would have you at my back anytime."

"Well, let's hope you don't need anyone there soon," said Tearlach. "I'm going to be away."

With a hearty hug, they parted ways.

Tearlach turned back to the ship which was almost fully loaded. He hurried down the dock, glad he had his favorite weapons with him, but wondering what he was going to do for clothes...

No one saw a second figure slip away from the docks and head back toward the castle by the shorter route.

* * *

Brodie made his way to the battlements following the route indicated by Ailean. He veered away only when the castle walls were clearly in sight. He took a major street running from the docks towards the castle and was almost to the entrance when he spied a man coming down the street from the castle towards him. The torchlights from the tower gate were at his back hiding his face in shadow.

Brodie approached with open hands showing he had no weapon.

"I have a message from Ailean and his cousin, Tearlach, for Chief Lachlan, are you a guard?"

The man seemed to stumble as he approached, and Brodie reached out to catch him.

The dagger stuck upwards swiftly striking just below the breastbone and driving up to the heart.

Stunned and shocked, Brodie looked down at the dagger in his chest, then he dropped to his knees.

"I'm sorry, Brodie, but that message must never be delivered."

As he fell forward and darkness closed his eyes forever, Brodie had a single thought.

"I know that voice..."

Chapter Five

A Challenge

Tearlach was getting sick of fish. They had been sailing for several days, heading south toward the coast of Ireland. The men were getting restless, bored, and weary.

The winds had been good the first day when they left the castle and had held for a day and a half before turning on them. They had been tacking back and forth ever since, a process that doubled the time it would take to reach the Irish coast.

A few of the men seemed to grumble more than others. Tearlach initially wrote it off to the lack of alcohol. Many of the men had joined the venture in their cups.

More than a few had spent the early morning hours of their flight heaving into the Atlantic's cold waters.

As time wore on however, he could see that the complaints were coming from a small cluster of men who seemed to know each other. Tearlach had a very uneasy feeling that there was a problem here that might only be solved with bloodshed.

They had skirted Mull, and the complainers said they should have stopped for more provisions, even though the ship was still well stocked. Ailean ignored them.

Tearlach could see from the heavy callused hands of all the sailors, that none of the men were strangers to the sea, or to rowing. In fact, his own were the least callused of the lot, except for Ailean's.

Tearlach was surprised at how well Ailean had taken command of the crew. Here his normally brusque manner of speech was taken as a sign of leadership. Still, it was only a matter of time until a challenge to his rule arose.

He wanted to talk to Ailean about it quietly, but there was nowhere private anywhere on a ship this small. He only hoped that the issue would come to a head soon and that Ailean knew it was coming.

He did not have long to wait.

The day started out badly. The seas were choppy during the night and the ship was making little progress against the waves. The morning dawned with a dense fog. They had already passed Islay, Ailean declining to turn back to Laggan Bay.

He was determined to reach the Irish coast.

A big man, Angus, seemed to be the leader of the complainers. He appeared to be gathering his courage. Ailean was watching the sea from the stern. The man stood with two others to back him. Tearlach was about to reach down for his axe when he felt a gentle poke in his back. He could feel a point positioned near his kidney.

"It's a knife," said a soft voice behind him.

"Don't turn around or it might poke harder. Let's let our new captain deal with his own choices, shall we?"

Tearlach froze.

Angus's voice was loud and gruff.

"I think we might be needing a new captain," he said.

Ailean's smile was almost friendly.

"And why would that be?"

"My friends here think that maybe a change of captains might bring a change of luck."

"So far, I'd say your luck has held pretty well," said Ailean, "I've let you bellyache for the past day and a half without cutting your throat."

Angus smiled in turn.

"Well that might be true, but I have three lads that will cast a vote for my being captain,"

He glanced at Tearlach, "including the one who has the knife to your friend's back."

Ailean's smile grew.

"Olaf? He was the first one of your band I spotted."

Ailean made a show of yawning.

"That's why I put two of my own behind him..."

Angus looked surprised.

Ailean's grin turned feral.

"I've been expecting a challenge since we left port. You were too eager to join. I've been waiting for you."

Ailean bent down and slowly uncovered a wicked looking axe that had been underneath an oilcloth next to his foot. The blade glinted from repeated polishing. He recognized it as the one from the axe toss contest.

Ailean winked at Tearlach.

"Hugh made the axe for me. I wanted

to see how well it was balanced. The contest was my idea. I put up the prize."

"Wish I was wearing it now," said Tearlach.

"You're a lousy swimmer to start with, and with that hauberk on you, you'd sink like a stone."

Ailean stood up, stretching lightly and picked up a small round shield that was under another cloth.

"Don't worry, I can handle this."

Ailean spun the axe in one hand.

"There's only three of them."

The men he faced had knives. For a moment, things were very still. Tearlach knew that Ailean was very good with an axe. His father insisted his sons know how to defend themselves. But in a fight with three against one a lot could happen. Tearlach felt the boat shift slightly. Other men were rising up, and it was clear Ailean wasn't bluffing. He had recruited others to his side.

It was going to be an ugly fight and while Tearlach was now sure how it would end, the ship would be shorthanded for a raid on the Irish coast.

It was then that Tearlach saw something coming out of the mists.

He tried to keep his voice very casual

as he spoke.

"Perhaps we should turn our attention to that ship over there and consider settling this matter afterwards?"

Chapter Six

First Prize

It was a wild hunt.

Initially becalmed like them, the ship recognized the danger it was in immediately and turned for the safety of the fog, her men rowing furiously. Ailean's men hesitated for a moment and a decision was reached when Angus suddenly sat and grabbed an oar.

"Plunder first!" he shouted. All the men roared approval and fell to their oars.

The small merchant birlinn managed to slip into the mists before they could catch up and in the dense fog it looked like they would escape.

But Ailean had his men quietly furl

the sail to help conceal their presence.
They drifted silently ears straining to hear.

It was Tearlach's keen hearing that caught the gentle lapping of a wave against wood. He signaled the direction to Ailean.

Ailean gave swift hand signals to his men. And they prepared to stoke on his command.

Ailean shouted.

"Starboard side stroke!"

Men responded instantly pulling together with practiced ease.

The ship turned swiftly, the rudder adding to the curve as the ship listed dangerously to one side with the violence of the turn. Tearlach could see that Ailean was smiling now.

"Both sides stroke!"

Now both sides pulled heavily and Tearlach bent his own back to the oar digging into the water and pulling hard.

The ship leaped forward.

He could hear men on the other ship now yelling.

"Both sides stroke!" called Ailean again.

Again, Tearlach and the others dipped heavily into the water pulling with all their strength.

He could feel the momentum of the

ship increasing.

The voices on the other ship were changing now, commands were being given.

He could hear the splash of oars entering the water.

They were almost to the other ship.

Looking up he could see Ailean at the stern of the ship, his eyes searching... Then, like a cat which has finally spotted its prey, he hunched forward, his chin jutting out.

"Both sides stroke!"

"What was he thinking? Was he going to ram the other craft? They could both sink!"

But there was no denying the authority in that voice. He, and the others bent their backs and pulled with all their might.

"Ship oars port!"

Tearlach and the other men responded instantly pulling their oars out of the water and raising straight them straight into the air.

At the same time Ailean leaned into the rudder and the ship began to turn.

Ailean was pushing against the rudder with all his strength pinning it to one side.

Through hissed breath he called,

"Starboard side stroke!"

On the other ship he could hear yells and confusion as Ailean's ship emerged from the fog right on top of them.

The last stroke of his ship pitted his crew against the rudder he was holding. The ship pushed forward turning only slightly as the bow of Ailean's ship came parallel to the other craft.

Ailean's ship ran straight alongside the other craft, smashing oars still in the water and driving them back into the rowers. Men screamed and cursed as their chests were smashed by the heavy oars and their thumbs and wrists cracked.

Ailean was up already and hurling a heavy grapple onto the smaller ship.

"Weapons!" Ailean called, and his men seized their axes and shields.

"Forward!" was the cry.

Men clambered across to the other birlinn.

And the slaughter began.

Photo 3 - A Birlinn

Chapter Seven

Second Prize

The merchant vessel limped along. There were several injured men in bloody clothes manning the oars. The ship itself showed signs of fighting.

The captain of the merchant cog that maneuvered to offer assistance was still wary. There was a fog not too far away that might at any second to reveal the pirates that this ship had obviously barely escaped from.

As he pulled alongside, he heard a call from one of his watchers.

Emerging from the mists was a fast moving birlinn under full sail. There were men waving axes in the prow and the captain could see a tall muscular hungry looking captain at the tiller.

"Raise sail!" he shouted and angled the rudder to flee this fast approaching menace.

It was then he saw the slow arc of a half dozen grapples coming from the wounded merchant to draw them together holding his ship from flight.

The birlinn would be on them in moments. Caught between the two ships he knew the outcome of the battle ahead.

He drew himself up, seized a shield and raised an axe.

Like wolves in a trap, his men would fight.

There would be no quarter, but he was descended from Celtic stock and did not hold with the Christian gods.

It would be a glorious battle and a worthy death.

He bellowed challenge and hurled himself aboard the merchant ship that had snared his fleet little craft.

He was met with ringing steel and as he fell, hacked by a half dozen blows, he prayed to his gods to forgive his foolish mistake and accept his honorable death.

* * *

Ailean was frowning.

Angus was abashed as he reported the results of the fray.

"We snared her with no problem. But that crazy Irish captain hurled himself onto our axes and caught poor Olaf in the chest with his own even as we cut him down. Never tried to defend himself, just flung his body into the fray. Used his shield to get Olaf's axe out of the way to strike.

I'm not even sure he lived long enough to know if his blow landed."

Ailean nodded.

"He knew."

Angus gulped.

"The rest of his crew went berserk then and we had a real fight on our hands until you came up alongside."

Ailean's face was calm and composed.

"How many did we lose?"

"Two dead and three seriously wounded."

Angus stepped closer.

"I don't think Malcolm is going to make it."

Tearlach stayed quiet, thinking. *"I could suggest returning now. No one knows what was done here. We could sink the merchant ships and return."*

He knew immediately that it was a childish dream. These were hard men. Men who drank and boasted of their deeds. Two days back in port and they would all be rounded up for the chopping block.

"We are going to need more men," said Ailean.

He turned to Angus.

"You wanted to be a captain. Do you still hold that dream?"

Angus eyed him carefully.

"I do."

"Good. I'm going to need captains. You see I'm not going to be a lone wolf prowling these waters. I'm going to gather and lead a pack. I'm going to take what I want - on the sea and on the land."

His face had that hard edge the Tearlach was coming to recognize as Ailean's true self.

"So, you can join me and be a captain, or I can get my axe and we can discuss your earlier suggestion that I'm not fit to lead."

Angus answered quickly.

"I don't like to admit I'm wrong. It's not in my nature. But I was wrong about you."

He straightened up and looked Ailean in the eyes.

"I'll follow you. And my men will follow you, too. And, if any of them says they won't... I'll gut them and bring you the entrails."

Ailean nodded.

"In that case, Captain Angus this will be your ship for now." He pointed to the newly captured merchant ship. We'll get you a better one soon. But I have a mission for you that requires this ship..."

Chapter Eight

Any Port in a Storm

Tearlach was set on lookout.

Angus had taken the merchant vessel with a hand-picked crew and returned to the castle at Duart to gather more recruits. There was little damage to the ship from the fighting and after the blood was washed off, she was ready to return to her role as a merchant vessel. Some of the less valuable loot was loaded on board to complete the impression.

Ailean had decided to set up a base not far from Cairn Na Burgh Mor and the Castle at Cairnburg where his grandfather, Iain MacLean of Treshnish, held sway. He knew the islands well from his childhood visits, which were frequent. He considered several locations, including Fladda and the Isle of Staffa further to the southwest, which had sheltered harbors and caves, but initially he decided that they would use a tiny island just to the west of Cairn Na Burgh Mor with a small bay and another island that partially sheltered it from storms to the north. The island could be dicey in a storm at high tide, but they should be fine for a while.

It was not ideal, but it would do until he could make a formal request to his grandfather.

He had no doubt that his ship would be seen approaching the isle, and he had little doubt that word of his "appropriation" would have reached his grandfather by now. He decided to approach the problem directly, arriving in his vessel with full sail, the sail of the MacLean's in full prominence.

A small vessel approached with a party of three.

They politely inquired as to the nature of the visit, and when told bluntly that Ailean intended to build and house a fleet to strike at the Irish coast, they raced off to inform his grandfather.

His grandfather sent back word that

he was invited to dinner that weekend.

* * *

Tearlach went with the party to the dinner. It was a quiet affair.

"Your father has disowned you," said his grandfather.

"And even your mother was upset at the murder of your cousin, Brodie."

Tearlach rose to protest, but Ailean held up a hand. His voice was surprisingly calm.

"And what did my father have to say?"

"Had he stayed a fortnight he would have been given the lands of Morven to govern and the estate at Killudine. Instead he has chosen the life of a freebooter and kinslayer. The ship he stole is his legacy now, and I hope never to see it's sail again."

"Ailean nodded, "As I expected. Always promising a better tomorrow and always delivering a slap today."

He looked at his grandfather.

There are many things I have ignored for the sake of my father's alliances. Hurts and slanders aplenty. No more! Tell my father I am no kinslayer. Brodie was not touched by me or any of my men."

"Is that all you would say?"

"No," said Ailean.

"Tell him this for me."

His face was red, and his hands trembled.

"From this point on, any who cross me — enemy, friend, or kin, I will kill. There will be no forgiveness, no letting it pass. And for those who have wronged me in the past..."

He stood and walked from the room. Over his shoulder the words came out harsh and biting.

"I will be coming for them."

* * *

"He's an angry, bitter man for one so young," said Iain.

Tearlach nodded. They were alone now. Everyone else had departed, even the servants were in the kitchens. Most of Tearlach's food still sat on his plate. His appetite was gone.

"He has the right."

Iain raised a single eyebrow.

"There's a tale here, I think. Can you tell it?"

Tearlach sat for a moment, considering.

"Yes," he said. "I think someone

should know, and I suspect that Lachlan will never hear the truth now."

Tearlach looked towards the door where Ailean had left.

"Bridges have been burned between father and son. But perhaps they might be maintained here."

And Tearlach told him the whole story, from beginning to end. He added his suspicions about the incident on the cliff and who was behind its spread.

Iain sat and listened, impassive, showing no reaction when Tearlach finished.

He rose slowly from the table and spoke.

"Ailean's freebooters may stay here, unmolested by me and mine, as long as no harm comes to my lands, those who trade with me, and MacLean ships."

His voice was deep rumble.

"Tell him that I'd prefer he hunt along the coasts of Ireland, but I suspect he plans to do that anyway."

He left by the same door as Ailean.

Tearlach was left with an empty room, a half-eaten meal, and a feeling that his old life was truly gone forever.

* * *

Ailean did not formally agree to his grandfather's terms, but his ships did not sail towards the Scottish coast. Angus was late returning, but when he arrived there was another birlinn, as well as his swift little merchant ship.

Both boats were filled with hard looking men. Tearlach recognized many of them. Second sons, the landless, orphans. Angus's net has been cast wide. Tearlach wondered at some of his choices. Because some, while hard, had no experience at sea. They had emerged green from the trip and kissed the ground as they left the ship.

Tearlach asked.

"Ailean's idea. 'Take any who want to be elsewhere and want a second chance. Some will be needed to build and maintain our holdings.' Thinking ahead, he is."

Tearlach caught his eye.

"Do you think he will succeed?"

Angus snorted and shook his head.

"Ambitious man. That's Ailean."

Angus face changed to a grim smile.

"He will succeed, or his death will be famous."

Then his eyes blinked, and he chuckled.

"Maybe both."

* * *

Eachann had been expecting Angus's arrival. He was surprised when his men reported that Angus had arrived in a merchant ship. He was even more surprised when Angus made no effort to contact him.

Eachann ordered his men to observe, quietly.

It was soon obvious that Angus was trying to recruit men to join him. And he wasn't being fussy about sailing experience. Eachann was curious. Was Ailean dead? Eachann had expected Angus to challenge him, he was the type. If so, where was the birlinn? Had Angus captured a prize and brought it to Duart? It showed more cunning than Eachann expected of him.

Perhaps it was his brother's hand behind all this? It seemed likely.

Eachann decided to be helpful. He ordered his men to scour the countryside for people who Angus might hire.

It was clear that Angus was looking for hard men. He rejected the drunks and hangers on sometimes driving them away violently. Those that remained were capable, tough, and looking for a way out of their present dismal condition.

In a very short amount of time, Angus had more "applicants" than his ship could hold.

Eachann decided to intervene again. He was sure that Ailean was alive, that he had a plan, and he was recruiting for an expedition of some kind.

Eachann smiled.

"With too many disgruntled men in your camp, you may find yourself quickly replaced."

Eachann rubbed his jaw.

"But how many was too many?"

He needed to act quickly before Lachlan became aware of the sudden influx of men outside his walls. Unless most were gone swiftly there would be inquiries.

He solved the problem elegantly.

There was an old birlinn near the end of the docks that was being repaired under his direction. He would report that the keel was cracked and the ship worthless. Then he would remove the guards who were normally guarding it and slip word to allow Angus to steal it.

In fact, it might be an opportunity to place a man into Ailean's circle. Someone who could be used later...

Chapter Nine

A Pirate's Mercy

Ailean's ship had caught the smaller merchant craft making its way along the Irish coast. It turned to flee but the larger sail and the bank of rowers of Ailean's ship made the flight a short one.

The battle was quick and bitter.

It was nearly over when he saw two men defending a third near the rudder of the other craft. The third man seemed slight of build and when he moved...

Ailean was sure.

He raced across the deck and leaped onto the other ship. His men were closing on the last of the defenders when Ailean ordered them to hold.

There was a stunned silence.

Ailean never spared any on a ship he took.

Tearlach was part of the boarding party and he came over to stand by his friend. His shirt was covered in blood and it dripped down his axe blade onto the deck.

The crew of the merchant vessel were all dead or dying.

Ailean casually drove his axe into a groaning man, killing him instantly.

"Be quiet. I wish to speak."

His men laughed but silenced quickly when he hefted the axe and looked around.

They had formed a semi-circle around the remaining defenders.

The defenders were clearly not crewmen. They had leather armor. Both were panting heavily, but gamely held their weapons and shields ready.

Behind them, the person they were defending was covered with a long robe, the hood drawn up.

As Ailean walked up his men parted.

"I see we have only three men left opposing us."

"We will fight to the last then and wait to watch you burn from the other side," said the man on his left.

"Ah," said Ailean. "Irish Christians you must be. By your speech."

"That's truth," said the man on the right.

"Is it?" said Ailean. Then he smiled. "Doesn't your god frown upon lies?"

"He does," said the man on the right.

Ailean gestured with his axe to the one in the back.

"Then shouldn't the lass have corrected me when I said it was three men?"

The two men shifted slightly.

Then with a swift move the hood was tossed back by its owner.

Her hair was fiery red, and her eyes were emerald green. Her face was smooth and not unattractive.

One of Ailean's men gave a low whistle. And there was a rumble among his crew.

Ailean spun the axe and they fell silent.

"What's your name, lass?" said Ailean and he gestured behind him.

"My men would like to know."

"It's none of their business."

"True," said Ailean. "But, if I loose them, they will make your acquaintance in other ways."

She brandished a small dagger.

"They won't have me alive," she replied.

"I'm sure some of them won't mind that at all," said Ailean mildly.

There were several hoots of laughter.

He raised his hand and they all fell silent.

"I'll trade you," said Ailean.

"My name is, Ailean MacLean, second son of Lachlan MacLean, Laird of Duart, and now a freebooter."

For a moment the woman looked confused at the formal introduction.

She decided.

"My name is Mary, Mary O'Brian"

Only Tearlach noticed the change in Ailean's face. Before, he had been a cat, playing with a mouse. Now, there was something else in his eyes.

Tearlach caught a grin on Ailean's face, then came a polite smile as if he were dancing with a lady at court. It seemed weirdly out of place.

"Thank you for your name, Mary O'Brian. For your courtesy, I will give you a gift."

He turned to face his men. His voice rose loud enough for all to hear.

"Except for those three, kill everyone

on this ship. Throw their bodies into the sea. Loot the ship, but do not damage it any further. The sail is torn and useless. Furl it and leave two oars so they can row.

He turned back to the three behind him.

"If these three try in any way to hinder you, kill the men, hack up their bodies for the fish, and you may have the woman any way you want."

He raised an eyebrow.

"Dead or alive."

He pointed.

"Those weapons of yours are loot as well as the armor."

The polite smile changed to an amused smile.

"You may keep the robe, lady."

There was an audible groan from one of his men.

He turned and began heading back towards his own vessel. As he walked away, he pointed casually at the man who groaned. The man was bald and missing several teeth. His body was short and pudgy, but his arms were massive. There was a mermaid tattoo that was scarred from a blade slash on his right arm.

"Mary, that is Calder. He is one of the ones who wouldn't mind dead."

Before he had taken a half dozen steps, he heard three weapons falling to the deck.

* * *

"We will have to do something about women," Ailean said, gesturing for Tearlach to take more ale.

Tearlach looked at him thoughtfully as he poured.

"They can be very disruptive. Whether you have them around, or you don't."

"Very true," said Ailean.

Ailean was picking at dirt under his thumb with a dagger. Tearlach recognized it as Mary's. Oddly, it was the only thing he claimed as his share from the ship.

His men had cleaned the ship out thoroughly just before nightfall. Tearlach had pointed the survivors in the direction of land and the two men had begun to row. Mary was at the tiller. The men rowed very badly. Tearlach could tell their hands would be blistered and useless for days by the time they reached the shore.

"Why did you let them go?"

Ailean grinned.

"It could be I was sentimental, swayed

by a name."

Tearlach looked at his friend.

"Somehow I don't think so. You may have fooled her into believing it was a romantic impulse, but I know better."

Ailean laughed openly.

"Caught me! It's true, there was a plan."

Ailean took a long drink and grinned.

"Eventually we had to take a ship with a woman on board. It was just luck her name was Mary. It did make the whole thing about letting her go more believable."

Tearlach nodded.

"So, why did you let her go?"

"Think, cousin! How can I grow a reputation and bring other pirates to me, if I kill everyone on every ship I encounter?"

Ailean took another swallow.

"Now I will be seen as dangerous, and impulsive. Other pirates will think they can use that against me if they join my fleet..."

"Fleet? You have four ships! And two are merchant ships."

"True," said Ailean, "but that one was useless. Too old and too slow. However, soon after they reach land, I will have more."

He emptied his tankard and placed it on the table.

"First, we let them see the soft leather of the glove. Then we let them feel the steel hidden beneath. Then they will come."

Chapter Ten

A Pirate's Cruelty

It was a hard chase.

The men were tired by the time they cornered the larger cog. Ailean leaned forward eagerly as the ship was cornered by the two birlinn's and grapples landed.

The men aboard the merchant ship were tired as well, but they knew that they were fighting for their lives. One had a bow and had been firing almost constantly since the ships came in range. He stood at the helm next to the tillerman. His aim was not great, but it kept Ailean's men busy.

Finally, when they got close enough, Tearlach jumped up shield in hand and hurled a throwing axe. The bowman, aiming at the prow of the Ailean's ship did not see it coming.

It landed with a solid thump that took him off his feet and dropped him over the side. Ailean's men roared approval.

But Tearlach was angry.

"Damn all the gods!" shouted Tearlach. "That was my favorite axe!"

"The waters a bit chilly, but you can feel free to go diving for it," Ailean shouted. "We'll be here for a bit and I can wait."

The laughter was brief and harsh, cut off by the shouts as men began clambering aboard the merchant ship.

The fighting was brutal, and screams cut the air as men died.

Ailean seemed to relish the sounds of battle, the cries of agony and death, but his eye was keen.

"Where is the captain?" He shouted.

"Cowering below!" shouted one of his men.

"Not likely," muttered Ailean jumping across to the other ship, axe in hand.

"With me!" he shouted and two of his men followed behind him.

Tearlach took a brief look at the helm, shook his head, and followed Ailean.

Ailean and his men found the merchant captain below the deck with a great axe in his hands, chopping away with all of his strength at the mast and keel of the ship.

He looked up when he saw Ailean.

"No damn pirate will have my ship!

He spat onto the floor and raised the axe to chop at the keel once again.

Ailean's axe flew through the air as the man's arms reached their apex. The blade cut deeply into his forearms just below his wrists, severing tendons, veins and muscle. The axe continued on, struck the side of the ship and stuck, dripping blood.

* * *

The merchant captain looked up in shock as he realized his hands were no longer under his control. His own axe clattered to the floor and he bent useless arms and gaped at wrists that flopped like useless things.

Then the pain hit him, and he howled in agony.

Above them the fighting had stopped except for the occasional thump of a finishing blow to a fallen sailor. Ailean had not spared anyone since Mary O'Brian and her companions.

"Take him topside," Ailean ordered, "and bring Leith down here if he didn't get himself killed in the fighting."

Men jumped forward and roughly hauled the merchant away. He tried to struggle and one of his men raised a dirk.

"No!" said Ailean. "I want him alive!"

The man stopped instantly and looked over to Ailean.

"Aye, captain."

And they dragged the crippled merchant up the stairs.

Leith appeared a short time later. He was a ship builder who fled his seaport village after killing his wife and son in a drunken rage. Angus had recruited him as he sat drowning his sorrows alone outside a gatehouse. Ailean had seen his value at once.

Leith looked at the damage and shook his head.

"We can shore up the damage and if we have good weather, she'll make it to port. But if we encounter any heavy weather the mast will crack, and the keel will fold."

Ailean's face darkened.

"Not encounter heavy weather this time of year? Might as well ask that it rain cooked beef so we don't have to start a fire!"

His voice was low.

"I wanted this ship. She has good lines. She's fast, and she's maneuverable. That captain has crossed me."

He looked up towards the stairs.

"He will pay."

He turned to the two men who had followed him below.

"Tie his arms to the tiller so he can steer."

He turned to Tearlach.

"Loot the ship quickly. Come to me when it is done."

Tearlach heard Ailean's voice as the climbed up.

"Leith, with me. There is something we must do."

* * *

Ailean and his men were all back aboard his ship. The other pirate vessel had taken a half share of the loot with them. It hovered nearby as the pirates gathered on both ships to see what Ailean was planning.

The grapples had been retrieved and the merchant ship drifted slightly.

Her captain, arms tied to the tiller, stood slightly hunched over glaring at

Ailean. His arms had been roughly
bandaged to prevent his bleeding to death.

"I'm giving you back your ship,
captain," Ailean shouted.

"She would have made a fine addition
to my fleet and you took that from me."

He shook his head.

"You should not have done that."

The merchant spat out a curse.

"Don't waste your breath," said
Ailean. "I've heard them all."

A few men chuckled.

"I'm sure you are wondering what I've
done."

His men looked expectantly.

"I've piled all the ballast of the ship on
the port side. Then I had Leith make a hole
about this big...

He held his hands to indicate a circle
about 3 inches in diameter.

"Just at the waterline on the aft side.

Of course, every wave brings a little
more water into the ship... making her list
even more to one side...

Oh yes, I also had Leith finish the
sabotage you were doing to the mast."

Ailean paused.

"The mast's weight should carry the
ship right over and snap off when she hits
the water. She should flip completely over

and float that way for several days. The current will carry her to land in a week or so.

But I'm afraid you won't be able to hold your breath quite that long, will you captain?"

Ailean turned and walked back to the aft of his ship and took the tiller. He steered his craft away while the merchant captain hurled feeble curses at him.

The ship was already beginning to sink, rolling slowly to port.

Tearlach was glad he did not have to watch the ending.

*   *   *

Ailean and Tearlach were drinking in the aft portion of the ship. The merchant had several kegs of ale and wine aboard and they had been divided among the men. However, the captain saved a special flask of brandy for himself and was sharing it with Tearlach now.

"Angus did well hemming that bird in," said Tearlach.

Ailean banged the railing with his fist.

"Damn! Why did I have to make an example with a good ship? Why couldn't it have been another fat lumbering beast like the one we let go?"

"Well, the men know that you are not to be crossed, that's a good thing," offered Tearlach.

"True, but I could have made the example just as well with a poor ship."

Ailean almost seemed to pout.

Tearlach laughed, trying to cheer his friend.

"Well, I guess you'll just have to go collect another good ship.

Ailean's head snapped up and down.

"Exactly. Signal Angus's vessel. Let's make for the Irish coast. We're going ashore. I need to gather another ship."

Photo 4 - A Merchant Cog

Chapter Eleven

Earning Respect

It was a scene of bloody carnage.

Ailean's plan was to catch the Irish clan unawares. They had only partly succeeded. A lookout had been able to cry out a warning before he fell from a low watchtower struck by Tearlach's thrown axe.

His men were past the palisade and among the Irishmen before they had gotten a chance to fully arm themselves.

But the fight was no easy one. Ailean placed several of his men along the shoreline to keep the Irish from the ship he sought.

Women and children fled into the

night though some grabbed weapons to join their men.

They fell with them.

Finally, only the Chieftain was left. The others had fled or been felled.

The big man had taken down two of Ailean's men, and while he was breathing heavily, he showed no signs of injury.

Ailean had taken a blow to his shoulder which was oozing blood through his leather.

Tearlach had to admit the Chieftain looked formidable. He was tall and muscular. His arms were covered with nicks and scars from past fights. He wore a leather chestpiece and cloak made from the fur of a large bear. He was older, probably at least forty and looked as if he'd reached that age by winning fights.

He stood now in the center of a tightening ring of men, like a lion surrounded by jackals.

But Ailean claimed his attention. He recognized the pirate leader and charged forward swinging the great claymore in his hands. Pirates jumped back avoiding the blade. Ailean did not. He took the blow on his shield and turned it up and away.

There followed an exchange of blows and Ailean's shield splintered under the force of his opponent's weapon. Despite its size and length, the Chief wielded it well, keeping Ailean from getting close enough to land a blow with his smaller axe.

"You fight well, Irishman,"

Ailean's men began to close around the big man, forming a circle.

He swung the claymore in a great arc pushing all the men away and replied.

"And you were doing well yourself, until you decided to hide behind your men's skirts."

Ailean stopped and stepped back.

"All of you stand clear."

Reluctantly the men fell back, Tearlach was the slowest to back away.

"You too, Tearlach," said Ailean.

He winked and faced the Chieftain.

"You have a large weapon there, Irishman."

The chief smiled.

"And you have a pretty face for a girl."

Ailean smiled.

"You try to goad me with that old insult? I'm afraid I will have to take that grin from your face, Chief."

Ailean twirled his axe.

"Let's see just how good you are, with your toy."

There was another exchange of blows.

Ailean was not able to get close enough to score while the big man fended off the smaller weapon and bashed Ailean's splintered shield so hard that it staggered him and almost took him to his knees.

They moved warily apart.

"Hah!" cried the chief. "Is that the best you can do? I'm surprised your mother gave you a ship to sail."

Ailean stood, his breathing was heavy. There was more blood oozing from his wound. He glanced back at Tearlach.

"All of you, listen to me. If he wins, he lives, keeps his ship, and all his belongings."

He turned back to the Chieftain.

"On my word."

"The word of a freebooter? What's that worth?"

"The word of Ailean MacLean of Clan MacLean."

The chief nodded.

"In that case Ailean MacLean, I promise to make your end swift. I'm going to cut that pretty grin right off your face."

"Really?" Ailean laughed.

Then he stopped, tossed away his battered shield, and his axe.

Tearlach gaped.

Ailean reached back and pulled out a

small dagger. Tearlach recognized it as the one he had taken from Mary O'Brian.

"The come on old man, let's play."

Tearlach expected some small retort, but instead the big man charged forward with surprising speed, covering the ground between them in two strides. The sword was up and swinging down in a huge arc intended to cut Ailean in half.

But Ailean was not there.

At the last second, he twisted to the side. He stepped in close, almost touching the big man's chest. And as the claymore descended the dagger drove up, under the armpit and into the chest of the big man.

The big man's arm closed trapping Ailean's hand and dagger. The hilt of the sword hit his injured shoulder.

Both men went down.

They lay collapsed together in the dirt for a moment. Then the big man rolled and rose on one arm. His claymore lay on the ground. Ailean struggled to his hands and knees. The chief coughed and blood gushed out. He whispered something to Ailean and collapsed. He did not move again.

Ailean nodded to the big man and rose.

He walked a few steps over and rolled

the big man on his back.

He pulled the dagger from his side wiped it on the chief's shirt and put it back in the leather sheath behind his back.

His men cheered.

He stood, looked around at the men.

"Take everything you can carry, but do not burn the huts..."

Tearlach walked over grinning to Ailean.

"Bold move. I didn't think that little sticker would reach his heart."

"I wasn't sure either. But a punctured lung would at least cut down on the jibes."

"Would you like help?

"No. The men must see me this way. Standing alone."

Tearlach nodded. He understood. It was respect Ailean sought from his men now. He would take chances to get it and take chances to keep it.

It was one of the prices of leadership.

"What did the big man say?"

"He asked that we leave the huts for the women and children. Winter will be cold."

Ailean shrugged.

"We'll scour the woods and take a few of the women back with us as prizes, but we'll leave the huts and the rest."

"Why?"

"A village of women will draw more men. They will bring more wealth with them and be even easier pickings when we come back in a year."

Ailean turned and walked away.

Tearlach nodded and turned back and began removing the heavy bearskin cloak and belt sheath from the Irish Chieftain for Ailean.

Chapter Twelve

Turning Point

Tearlach had gathered all the men together as Ailean had ordered. They had been camped on the coast for an evening using the birlinns turned on their sides for shelter against the wind. Campfires were burning low. They were a disorderly lot by nature and there was a bit of jostling before they were all gathered and ready.

Ailean appeared carrying his axe and looked from man to man. Sound died rapidly. When the sound of waves was all that could be heard, he spoke.

"Up to now we have been preying on the shipping along the shores of the Irish Coast. And while the rewards have been ample..."

His men laughed as Ailean leaned down and patted the large stomach of the cook, Ewen.

"...The travel to and from that Coast is a long stretch. There are storms and the possibility of running into other pirates when our own forces are depleted."

He saw men nodding.

"Our ranks are increasing and our location here will not stay hidden much longer.'

"And with bad weather coming we need a better shelter than one that could be underwater with the right tide and storm."

"What do you propose?" said Tearlach, on cue.

"We have the forces to take an estate and hold it. I propose we seize one and hold it through the winter. By spring people will have accepted it as ours and we are less likely to have to fight to keep it."

"Won't we lose a lot of men?" said Tearlach.

"Not if we are smart and pick the right estate," was Ailean's reply.

"A large estate that is poorly defended, near the coast so we can anchor our ships and make repairs."

"Do you know of an estate like that?"

said Angus.

"I do. And it is ripe to be plucked."

Ailean held up his hands. The room was silent.

I propose we go to Lehire and take away the estate at Torloisk from that doddering old man, Neil.

There was some quiet rumbling. Ailean waited for a moment.

It was the cook who swayed the crowd. His voice was loud and carried well.

"Well, captain you have the devil's own luck at sea. I'm curious as to how you will fare on dry land. I'll follow you."

Then he gave a loud barking laugh.

"Besides, I'd like to add some beef to my diet, and I hear Lehire has some fine cattle."

There was a roar of approval at that, followed by shouts of warm beds, ale, and women for the taking.

Ailean was smiling.

"I take it you all are with me then?"

"Aye!" was the loud thundering response.

Ailean whipped out his axe and brought it down is a thundering crunch on the table. His men froze.

"In a fortnight we set sail for Torloisk!" shouted Ailean, "For plunder and glory!"

"And beef!" shouted Ewen and they all laughed.

Only Tearlach, who was watching Ailean carefully, saw him smile and softly mouth the words.

"And revenge."

Chapter Thirteen

Nan Sop

Tearlach had heard the story from some of those who tormented Ailean at Duart. When he was seven, Neil, Chieftain of Lehire, had scalded him with boiling water. The boy, caught by surprise and pain, burst into tears and ran to his mother. The Chieftain then made fun of his tears, and running away, saying a real man wouldn't scream at a little heat.

* * *

Ailean's men struck just before dawn. They drove towards the estate of Torloisk sweeping foes aside. Neil, much older now, gave ground steadily, his men falling back toward the manor house. Finally, they were driven behind the walls of the house.

Ailean's frustration gradually turned into rage. He tried repeatedly to reach Neil, to corner him into a fight, but other warriors always came between them.

Finally, with the remainder of Neil's forces forced into the manor house, Ailean's men began to look for a way in.

Tearlach watched as Ailean, his face red, his eyes bright, fumed as ladders, and even a battering ram were repulsed.

His annoyance growing, he looked around the lands he came to seize.

Out in the fields he spied several giant bound hay wheels. When completely dry, the round wheels were normally rolled into the manor's barns. This would happen later in the year and supply feed for the cows during the winter months.

Ailean directed several of his men to bring up several of the wheels and place them against the sides of the manor house, blocking off the arrow slits in the lower windows.

Ailean's men kept those on the rooftop pinned down with poor archery. The sailors were not bowmen, but with enough people shooting allowed his men to get close and place the hay wheels. Finally, a wagon loaded with hay was pushed up to the front gate.

When the building was surrounded by straw, Ailean and his men fired flaming arrows at the stacks. Soon the outer walls were encased with fire and heavy black smoke.

Tearlach waited with the others to see what would happen. Would the men inside simply die of the smoke or would they come out to fight?

There was a grating sound near the gate. Men pushed against the wagon and stumbled over the burning straw to stagger out. Blinded from smoke and scorched form the heat they held weapons for a last desperate battle.

Tearlach saw a figure near the back exhorting his men to greater effort and then coughing and wheezing he came through the gate himself.

Ailean was there to meet him.

The old man looked at him with hate filled eyes.

Ailean looked amused.

"When I was a child you told me that tears were for babies and not real men. You told me that only cowards run away. Yet you ran away from me and my men...

When I look, I see tears on your eyes! And, you flee your home? Only to come limping out a little while later? Are you afraid of a little heat? Come, let us see who is the real man now."

Enraged, Neil came at Ailean with axe and shield.

They traded blows for a few minutes, while around him, Neil's men fell one by one.

There were only a few left now.

Most of Ailean's men, had stopped fighting so they could watch the duel.

Another round of blows was exchanged.

Tearlach could see that Ailean was simply defending, conserving his strength. Neil was growing more tired by the minute as he launched attack after attack, while Ailean circled, calling him child, baby, and coward.

Neil was almost exhausted when Ailean jumped back and shouted.

"Enough! I wanted your men to see how weak and pathetic you are. I haven't even been trying, while you flail about like the doddering old fool you are! Now listen to me men of Lehire! After I kill this wretch, any of you who lays down his arms will be spared - as will your family. You will work for me as you did your pathetic master. For those who do not, neither your lives nor the lives of your wives and children will be spared. Think on your choice.

Neil roared in rage and charged.

Ailean waited calmly. Neil feinted with his axe and tried to slam Ailean with his shield.

Ailean was not fooled.

As the shield came at him Ailean, lowered his body quickly, braced himself, and brought his shield up to meet the blow. Shields smashed into each other. Ailean took the full force of the blow without moving an inch. Neil staggered back as if hitting a stone wall. As he staggered back his arms went wide for balance.

Ailean's axe flew from his hand straight into Neil's chest. The force of the blow took the man completely off his feet and he landed on his back, the blade buried deep.

Neil screamed.

As he fell, Ailean laughed. Then spoke his voice cold and vicious.

"Oh, you scream in pain, do you? It seems we have come full circle. But I don't see your mother and you make far too much noise..."

He stepped forward and drove his

shield into the dying man's throat. There was a snap as the man's neck was broken by the force of the blow. The screams stopped and the body began to tremble and shake as the limbs flailed with no brain to command them.

Ailean stood watching impassively until they stopped. He bent down and pulled the axe from Neil's body.

He held up the bloody axe.

"Men of Lehire, choose your fate! Serve me or serve with your families in hell!"

His voice rose to a shout.

"Now, I rule! I am the MacLean of Torloisk!"

*   *   *

"We have his son," said Tearlach.

Ailean raised an eyebrow.

"Where is he?" said Ailean.

Tearlach jerked his head towards the open gate.

"He was wounded and was captured by the men."

"Captured? Why would they capture him?"

"They thought he might be good for ransom."

105

Ailean nodded.

"Normally a good thought," he conceded.

"Where is he now?"

"Angus and another man hold him over by the gate."

Ailean turned and walked toward the gate. Strolling past burning huts, he breathed in the smell of burning straw and human flesh with no signs of discomfort.

As he got closer, he could see Angus and another pirate standing over a man, hunched in the dirt.

"Did he put up much of a fight?"

Angus shrugged.

"Nothing to speak of."

Ailean's axe came down and split his skull in a single swift motion.

"It was a good idea to take him as hostage Angus, except there will be no one left to ransom him to."

The body fell over and slumped in the dirt. Brains and blood oozed out onto the sand.

Ailean bent down and wrenched his axe from the man's skull. He straightened slowly and swung the axe in a vicious downward arc to clean it. Looking up, he gestured at Angus and the man standing with him.

"Now, get out there and get some loot before it's all gone."

He pointed at an unburned hut.

"I believe I saw women running into that one a few minutes ago. It probably has a hidden bolt hole in the floor. Have some fun and maybe they will have some plunder as well. They had time to hide it with them."

Angus grinned and he and the other man sprinted towards the hut. Soon there were screams of pain and terror and growls from the men.

Ailean turned to Tearlach and gestured at the body on the ground and then looked over at the hut.

"A small reward, Tearlach. It wasn't the best of ideas, but Angus is learning to think a bit more, at least."

Chapter Fourteen

Pirate Laird

Tearlach was sweating from hours of labor. He and the other men had been working to bring in as much of the harvest as possible before the coming of winter.

The pirates had grumbled, but when it was pointed out that without the harvest there would be no beef, no ale, and no point in staying, they fell to.

There was also work to be done strengthening the defenses of the manor, setting up watches to be prepared for a strike by any who felt they had a grievance against the pirates. It was a long list.

There was also the issue of keeping an eye on new people coming aboard.

Pirates are not a trusting lot by nature and the process of proving oneself to Ailean became more difficult as time went on. His men were ruthless, sadistic, and cold. And to lead them Ailean became harder than all of them.

Tearlach felt he liked it that way. It was a challenge. And Ailean had found his home. Not with Torloisk, that was just a way station, Tearlach was sure, but with the life of a freebooter. It was a life in which you looked out for yourself, trusted no one too deeply, and went after whatever you wanted with total focus.

That was Ailean's life from an early age and in finding others who thought like him he found a strange kind of family.

Tearlach worked hard to keep his fighting skills up, because he never knew when he might provoke another pirate into a fight.

He had already killed two others over petty matters.

The fights were as fair as pirate fights ever are. He put his back to a wall and watched for friends who might tilt the scales. He never asked or used his friendship with Ailean as a lever. It would have shown weakness and been a death sentence.

Ailean's men despised weakness over everything. They loved Ailean's ruthlessness, his bravado, and his willingness to take chances. Most of all they loved that he won. All the attitude in the world is worthless if you don't win. In a pirate's world winning means being alive to pillage and plunder when the fighting is over.

So far, Ailean had delivered every time.

Of course, he only had to fail once. When that happened, his own men could turn on him like jackals after an old crippled lion.

But, Ailean wasn't old or crippled yet, and Tearlach intended to keep him that way.

After the fire around the manor was put out Tearlach and some men went in and cleaned out the bodies of the women and children who had perished inside. Only a handful of Neil's men had surrendered, and true to his word, they and their families had been spared.

There had been a certain amount of rape, plunder, and pillaging after taking the manor and nearby village, but it was relatively mild. Ailean wanted those who worked the farms and did the routine work still alive to help maintain the place.

They all became servants of course. Those that refused were immediately executed, regardless of status or occupation.

The manor and surrounding lands had become a haven for pirates, and pirates knew that if they joined Ailean they could look forward to that safe harbor.

There were some rules. Certain ships were never to be touched. Any that bore the mark of Duart on their sails were safe, as were the sails of his grandfather's ships. There were also exemptions for sails from areas allied with his father and grandfather.

As the number of vessels Ailean captured grew so did the ranks of his men. He was becoming a legend among the pirates and feared by those who sailed the Irish shores.

Tearlach knew the time was approaching when Ailean would begin to expand where he hunted. And, he had demonstrated that he wasn't above taking and holding territory.

But even Tearlach was surprised by Ailean's next move...

Chapter Fifteen

Pirate Conqueror

Winter was almost over.

Ailean's men were restless and irritable. Ailean was no better. Over the colder months, men had come to join the pirate group - men who were untested. There were a lot of them.

Tearlach looked at them and thought most would not survive a single fight. But Ailean welcomed them all, gathered them and ordered his men to give them some training.

The snows were still flying when he announced that they were going to take all the lands surrounding Torloisk. The men smiled. The veterans understood.

It was time to separate the wheat.

Ailean's veterans went on the ships to strike from the sea. His new recruits struck from the land. At each town the same choices were usually offered.

"Bend knee or bend your neck," he'd call out.

"I'll have your allegiance, or I'll have your head."

Some offered serious resistance. Ailean slaughtered them wholesale, burning the huts, usually with the occupants inside. By fall, he was using hay from the farmer's fields to roast the recalcitrant.

"A good example today, means I might not have to level a whole village tomorrow," he told Tearlach.

The villages fell, one by one.

Chapter Sixteen

Hunting Pirates

"We're hunting pirates?"

We stood around a long table in an area of the mansion Ailean had claimed for planning. The table was long so large maps could be spread, and the light from several torches around the room made viewing good. The room had only one entrance and had solid walls on all sides. There were no windows, it was in the center of the manor. Fireplaces on either side of the room had extra vents to draw of the torches smoke.

Ailean liked it because it allowed him to concentrate without petty distractions and no one could enter without being seen. He kept a man posted at the door and to approach you had to go down a narrow corridor.

I know my mouth hung open like a landed fish, but I knew I wasn't alone.

That's right, we are hunting pirates," said Ailean calmly.

Angus looked ready to burst.

"Why would we do that?" he said. "They are better armed than merchant ships, they have fast ships that will be hard to catch, and they have captains who will be wise to most of our tricks."

Ailean frowned. He did not like having his orders questioned. Tearlach realized that Angus was walking on very dangerous ground.

Angus seemed to sense it too. He backpedaled carefully.

"I'm sure the men will want to know. Some of them may even have former comrades on those ships."

Ailean relaxed slightly, but his face still clearly showed his annoyance. He straightened and took a deep breath. His shoulders relaxed slightly, and he smiled as he spoke.

"First, they are taking prizes away from our vessels.

Second, they are attacking vessels that I have given orders not to strike."

Like a sudden storm cloud appearing over a mountain, his face changed. The look he gave Angus made the man take a step back.

"This is my sea! I rule it! Those merchant ships are my prey and no one else's!"

Then, in an instant, the anger was gone, and the smile returned.

"Third, and most important.

They have not joined my fleet. I mean to recruit most of those men and those ships to my fleet, or I will send them to the bottom of the sea."

He bent forward and his hand slapped the desk between them.

"These are my orders. Close on a ship so it is clear you can catch her. Offer the choice. Join my fleet or be sunk. If a captain refuses her men can pick a new captain or they can all go down with him.

For any ship that joins us with a captain. Bring him back so I can meet him personally."

He smiled.

"His crew might need a new captain if I decide he is playing games...

If part of a crew decides a new captain is in order, board and take out any who opposed the switch.

Then bring the ship back to me. I'll want to meet the new captain and see if he needs 'assistance' in his job. We will put a few of our men on every new ship.

Finally, if any ship opposes me. Kill her crew to the last man. Tie their bodies on their wooden shields and toss them in the ocean. The bodies will float longer and leave a message for future crews to make better choices."

* * *

It didn't take long to get results. New ships began to appear at the harbor. There weren't a lot of pirates out there and they soon got the message. A few shifted hunting grounds which was fine with Ailean. A couple joined; one was sunk. Within three months Ailean was alone in much of the area where his men preyed.

His fleet had grown to twelve fast ships and many smaller vessels. Some of those that joined him had old merchant birlinns that were beached by Leith for parts. The number of men on his ships swelled. His own was still fastest of all. Of that he was secretly proud.

But now that he had a fleet, he needed to change tactics. He had only made a few forays in Ireland on land. With more men and ships his forays could increase.

His days of trying to capture ships at sea was ending. It was too time consuming and too chancy. It was time to expand. He wasn't sure where he should strike first, but he knew that with the force he now commanded that he needed to strike soon. His men would grow restless without action and the amount of food that so many men would consume would tax the lands he had so recently acquired.

What he did not know was that events were taking him towards that goal in a wholly unexpected way.

Chapter Seventeen

Second Thoughts

Eachann was in a quandary. His father's ships had stopped having trouble with pirates. His father had replied by not sending anyone against his son after the seizing of Torloisk.

Ailean was proving to be a much cannier individual than Eachann expected. Still, he was in line for the Chieftainship and while Eachann was first in line there were always accidents that could happen. Family politics was a strange business. On the one hand, Eachann liked his little brother. He was a bit of a berserker as Eachann remembered him, but he could suppress his rages. He definitely was one to hold a grudge, even after the slight should have passed.

His father was also seeing a falling of influence in those who were not allied with Duart. This was because they were now feeling the pinch of Ailean's actions.

He had amassed enough men to start doing raids and several had proved devastating.

Eachann sighed. He was going to have to think on the problem of his brother a bit more. A deeper plan than before. Perhaps he could point his brother at someone and let word slip out?

Something to think about. He needed more information.

* * *

The man was visibly shaking in his presence.

"A good beginning," thought Eachann.

His face was hard.

"My father is away, and I am in charge. What's your name?"

The man's voice was soft and trembling.

"Glenn."

"You have been charged with petty theft. How do you plead?"

The thief dropped to both knees and sobbed.

"It was a loaf of bread, my Laird. It was moldy, the baker put it out and I thought it was going to the slops. I was hungry. I haven't eaten in two days."

"Indeed, the man was skinny, bones really," thought Eachann.

He looked to the baker.

"What's your side of this?"

The baker nodded.

"It's just as he says. The bread was moldy. It was going to my hogs. But it was my bread and my hogs who got shorted a meal!"

Eachann nodded.

He looked back to the skinny wretch.

"So, you both agree on the circumstances. That makes it very easy."

He looked at the skinny man making his face completely impassive.

"You are guilty of petty theft. The penalty is the loss of a hand."

The thief wrung his hands together and began clutching at his wrists as if one hand were already gone.

"No! My laird, please, no!"

But Eachann wasn't watching the thief. He was watching the baker, whose face paled visibly.

Two men came and seized the thin man they began to drag him away.

The thief was screaming now in fear.

The baker looked up at Eachann who was watching him intently.

"My laird, if I might, I would withdraw the charges…"

Eachann smiled.

"Exactly as I predicted…" he thought.

"Why would you do that?" he asked.

"I was angry at the loss, but I don't want that man to lose his hand over a loaf of bread destined for pigs."

"They were your pigs," Eachann remarked calmly.

"Yes, and I feed them well. A loaf of bread less won't hurt them none."

His men had stopped at a silent signal holding the unfortunate thief.

"Still the law must be observed. Thieves must be punished."

He looked over to the thief who was collapsed on the floor, sobbing.

"I will give you a chance to redeem yourself, thief."

The man fought to stop sobbing and looked up hopefully.

"I want you to deliver a message to my brother. Do this and return with his reply and your sentence will be revoked."

Yes, my Laird.

"Can you read, thief?"

"No, my Laird."

"*Better and better,*" thought Eachann.

"I will give you a letter to deliver. Make sure it is given only to my brother. I will arrange passage for you to Torloisk."

His face grew stern.

"And when you return, I will have questions for you. Be observant."

"Yes, chief."

* * *

Amazingly the thief actually returned. Eachann had expected that the pirates would simply kill the stupid man and then deliver the message when they searched his body.

The thief's tale almost went that way. The pirates fell on his undermanned birlinn in the early morning hours. Her captain did not see the heavily armed ships until they stood no chance of getting away.

"*They must have been surprised that their prey steered towards them instead of away,*" thought Eachann.

They were swiftly flanked, and men looked ready to pounce, but his cries of message for Ailean caused one of their captains to hesitate.

"And what captain was this?" Eachann asked.

"His name was Tearlach," said the thief.

The man looked apologetic.

"They said they had not heard of your safe passage guarantee from Ailean..."

Eachann said nothing.

That the idiot still thought Eachann placed any value on his life amazed him.

"The gullibility of some people..."

Eachann had sent a simple message with the details of the family and a warning that his father had not cooled down. He added that the Lachlan had not ordered any attempt to retake the estates which Ailean now held. That would be useful information for his brother.

The thief held a written reply.

The reply from Ailean was surprising. It detailed a simple flag signal that was to be put on his ships. If seen by his men, his ships would not be bothered. Also, Ailean detailed lands that his men would not attack.

This was more than he could have hoped for. He planned to bargain with Ailean for safe passage and protection of key territories. But his brother was giving him the rights for free!

Eachann looked up from the message.

"How many ships did you see?"

"Three. There were the two that met us, and one was beached on the shore. How many were at sea I could not tell."

"Good. And how many men?"

About forty. There were women as well. And the estate was being tended by several lads. I saw about a half dozen working in the field with some girls, and a few who were tending to the cattle.

He smiled.

"The cook was very good at cooking beef! The men were well fed and looked healthy, although many were scarred.

"And how did Ailean look."

"He was in good health. He sat at the head of the table and ate well. He did not drink much, but let his men drink their fill."

"I see. And how did his men view him?"

The thief's gaze seemed to drift for a moment.

"Frankly, his men looked like they would follow him into battle at the jaws of hell. And," he added, "they just might win."

"You have done well."

Eachann thought for a moment.

"Your crime is forgiven. You may return to your family."

"I have none. They are all gone."

"In that case, if you are willing I shall use you again as a messenger. You will get food and lodging in the village, but you will avoid any contact with anyone else in my family. Is that clear? If I have a message for you to deliver, I will send someone for you."

The man nodded.

Eachann considered.

"A man alone with no visible source of income will cause talk. Apprentice yourself to the baker. I will assure that he accepts you. It will give you money for ale."

Eachann's voice grew hard.

"But take care that you do not drink too much. If one word of your service to me ever reaches my ears..."

He did not have to finish the statement. He could see the man shaking even at a distance.

"Go, find lodging in town. I will send word to the baker to hire you. Make sure you earn your keep. If his profits fall, he may talk."

The thief nodded and hurried out.

Eachann sat and thought for a long while.

"Ailean's forces are not a threat to me

as long as I am not caught by surprise. And Ailean still seems to not have a suspicious bone in his body where I am concerned. He still seems to be trying to win me to his side..."

Eachann smiled.

"For now, that is good enough. However, I need to point his energies in a new direction."

However, fate was already stepping in to help him.

Chapter Eighteen

A Murder in Edinburgh

"How did he die?"

Ailean sat rigid. His face a stoic mask.

His grandfather sighed.

Lachlan went to Edinburgh under safe passage from the Earl. He was staying at the castle in Edinburgh. According to reports, John Campbell of Calder and six of his men attacked and slew him in his bed. He claimed it was in retribution for dishonoring his sister, Catherine, whom your father tried to drown to get out of his marriage.

Ailean stayed calm.

"She did try to poison him first..."

Iain smiled.

"Political marriages often have their little issues."

Tearlach, who was listening from further down the table nodded.

Ailean frowned.

"The Earl of Argyll is behind it all," he said.

"Likely true," Iain replied.

Iain leaned back away from the table and patted his stomach.

"John is hotheaded and a few well-placed words from the Earl and he would likely have gone off and done something rash."

"There will be an accounting," said Ailean.

He straightened and put down his cup.

"But first, I have a duty."

He turned to Tearlach.

"I want every ship in the fleet ready to go by tomorrow. We sail for Duart."

"Your brother, Eachann, will be made Chieftain now," said his grandfather.

Ailean's voice was surprisingly quiet.

"It's not for my brother I sail. It is for the memory of my father."

* * *

Ailean stood before over a hundred men. He had lost track of the exact number. They rose and fell as his raids along the Irish Coast had increased. Battle had losses. Plunder drew recruits.

He raised his axe and all the men fell silent.

His voice was loud, deep, and menacing.

"The Earl of Argyll and those who follow him have offered me a grave insult."

He smiled and his voice grew light.

"But we are freebooters! What is an insult to us?"

He gave a little shrug and there was a low grumble.

He feigned surprise.

"Oh, I see a bit of dissent among you."

He paused. Then he began to speak. His voice grew harsher as he went on and a bit of the rage he felt came out. His face reddened and his voice went from soft and timid to a roar.

"I share your dissent. I am Ailean MacLean of Clan MacLean. No one — man, woman, or beast in the field challenges me without reply."

He spit on the ground.

The Earl's ships are now fair game.

And I will offer my share as an extra prize to any who bring me proof of a capture or sinking.

"But that is far from enough! Argyll lands are now fair game. We no longer face the long sail to the Coast of Ireland for plunder! Argyll lands will provide all we need."

His head turned.

"Tearlach are the ships ready?"

"They are," was his quick reply.

Ailean face turned back to his men.

"We sail to Mull and Duart to pay my respects. Then we sail for the nearest Argyll lands to see what their cattle, ale, and women taste like."

The men roared approval and raced to their boats.

Ailean drew close to Tearlach.

"Did you make the special preparations I asked for?"

Tearlach smiled.

"I did. I had the women work on it all night."

"And the flags?"

"One black flag on the top of each mast. I put them there myself."

Ailean nodded.

"Then let's get underway."

He waded into the water, vaulted

aboard his ship, and strode to the helm.

Tearlach took his place among the rowers.

The ship pulled out into the lead quickly, followed by Angus's birlinn and five others. Behind them came a bevy of merchant ships that Ailean had captured and kept. Fighter or not, almost every man in Torloisk had been stripped for the trip. They numbered in the hundreds.

The reached a point where the winds began to pick up.

"Raise sail!" Ailean ordered.

And quickly the sail came up, a revised sail, one made for the occasion. On it was the family crest of the Clan MacLean. But now, the edges of the sail were bordered in black.

Other sails billowed out and the fleet moved swiftly out into the ocean and turned towards Mull.

* * *

Ailean's ships formed a "V" with his ship in the lead. They drew swiftly towards the coast of Mull. They sailed openly up the coast in sight of land drawing close to Duart Castle.

Ailean was sure his brother and his

mother could see him from the battlements. He stopped his ships short of the shore and had all but his ship drop their sails.

The small black banners atop each mast and the black border around his sail was the message he wished to give his mother.

"*My father,*" he thought, "*will be avenged tenfold.*"

* * *

Eachann stood next to his mother and looked at the fleet of ships that floated just offshore.

"*So many ships and men! I had no idea! My brother has become a force to reckon with!*"

Next to him, his mother looked at the ships. All but one had furled its sail and rested. The lone ship had a large sail bordered in black. All that held it back was the heavy anchor which had grabbed some undersea protrusion. The family crest of Clan Maclean billowed in its sail. It looked like a beast straining against the chain holding it back.

Marion, his mother, stood quietly looking at the scene then she turned to her servants.

"Bring me wood. Enough for a bonfire - pile it here in the center of the tower. I want enough that it can be seen clearly by those ships..."

Eachann nodded to several of his retainers and pointed to his mother's servants.

"Help them. I want the wood piled twice the height of a man. Make it dry so it will burn brightly."

He smiled at her.

"The prodigal asks for permission, mother. He wants to strike back to avenge his father."

She nodded.

"I know. He shall have it," she said.

She looked at Eachann with a cool, measured gaze.

"And he was never a 'prodigal' in my eyes."

Eachann said nothing.

She glanced away to the ships, then back to her eldest son.

"They call him 'Nan Sop' do they not?"

Eachann nodded.

She turned to a favorite guard who accompanied her almost everywhere.

"I want you to take a message to the ship that still has its sail out.

She pointed."

134

"Do you see it?"

The man nodded.

"Good."

She carefully removed a ring from her right hand.

"Take this ring. Fill the center with fresh straw and bring it to that ship. Give it to the captain."

The man nodded.

"Are there any words you wish to go with the ring?"

She nodded.

"Yes. Tell him to do what he does best to the enemies of Duart and my husband's murderers. He has his mother's blessing."

*　*　*

It was almost dark. Against the setting sun Marion stood quietly while the final preparations were made for the bonfire. As the last edge of the sun fell below the horizon, Marion called for a torch.

She stood quietly as it was brought. Eachann stood next to her.

All day the winds had blown. All day the ship had strained against the anchor. Not a sound had come from any vessel moored before the castle.

The guard had returned just a few minutes before. He stood quietly next to her.

"Did you deliver my message""

"I did my lady."

She did not ask if he had replied. Instead she walked to the pyre holding the torch high. She hurled the torch into the center of the fire. Flames crawled upwards as the dry wood caught fire. Soon a blazing pyre sent flames leaping twenty feet into the air. The sky was turning dark, but she could still clearly see the ships.

One by one, torches were lit from the helm of every vessel.

And then, the ship which had been straining all day against the anchor suddenly broke free as the anchor was released.

The ship heeled around sharply and raced out to sea turning in an arc that brought it close to shore.

Marion could see a tall, muscular figure at the helm. One hand on the tiller the other holding a torch.

Sails raised on the other ships and they turned following their leader out to sea. At the helm of every ship was a warrior with a torch in one hand and a hand on the tiller.

As the ships departed, she could hear the men beating their shields in time.

It was time to set the seas ablaze with vengeance.

Marion walked from the burning pyre to her rooms. There she would mourn the loss of her husband.

* * *

Eachann watched the departing fleet. He would never have believed that his brother could inspire such loyalty or command such respect from rogues and pirates.

"My brother goes to make war," he thought. "And I shall not be far behind."

He gestured to a guard.

"Double the guards on the battlements," he ordered. "Gather messengers and send them to the council chambers. We will call our allies and strike at Campbell lands before month's end."

He looked out at the ships fading rapidly in the distance.

"Lachlan will be doubly avenged."

Chapter Nineteen

The Fall of Mingarry

The assault had been swift and decisive. Men lay dead and dying from the gate all the way to the main tower, and up the stairs to the bedroom of the MacIan chief, their cries being cut short by the axes of the pirates and they made sure of their victory.

Ailean stood on the top of the battlements looking out over the sea, ignoring the battle that raged below him. The battle was already over — the defenders of Mingarry just didn't know it yet.

He had already slain the MacIan Laird, another of his detractors, as the man raced from his bedroom to defend the castle.

"At least he had a sword in his hand when you cut him down," said Tearlach.

"It hardly mattered. He was barely awake, and you could smell the alcohol the length of a room away..."

Tearlach asked the question gently.

"And the babe?"

Ailean was diffident.

"She threw it off the battlements to the rocks below. The body washed out to sea."

Tearlach nodded.

"At least you didn't have to do it."

Tearlach looked around.

"And where is the wife?"

"God knows. She went even crazier when I spurned her. Claimed I made her kill the babe. After we secure the village and castle, I suspect the tale will grow like wildfire."

"Well it would be like you, 'Nan Sop'," said Tearlach.

"As if I was the only man who ever burned out a building with a few people inside it!" said Ailean.

He sighed.

"You would think I invented fire and straw the way the damn story goes now."

Tearlach looked seriously at his friend.

"Well, you do use it a lot..."

"It works!" said Ailean irritably. Then he grinned.

"You're poking fun at me, aren't you?"

Tearlach laughed.

"Caught me," he admitted. "But what are you going to do about the wife?"

"Nothing," said Ailean. "The story will be told regardless."

"Well, you did encourage her affections."

"Of course, I did! This is a perfect next step for us! A defensible castle, a place to moor our ships without having to drag them inland. More land under our control, and best of all.

His face went cold.

"A slap in the face to Argyll."

Ailean paced across the battlement looking out to sea and thinking.

He turned.

"Tearlach, make sure that woman gets out alive. I don't want any of our men to harm her."

"Getting soft?" said Tearlach.

Ailean snorted and spat.

"Of course not! But there is a way to spin this in my favor. This is the story I want to circulate..."

And he outlined the plan.

"You will spread the word that I told the woman she must throw the babe off the battlements to the rocks below to assure that the people would follow me. She resisted twice saying the child was looking at her and laughing. Finally, I told her not to look at the child, but to turn her head. After the child was gone, I repudiated her and drove her from the castle saying that if she could kill her child, I could not trust her not to kill me."

When he was done Tearlach shook his head.

"Well we can tell the story that way, but I don't see how it gets you anything."

"Oh, there are many who remember the story of Solomon and the babes. This will stand their Bibles on end! The best part is - it is mostly true."

Tearlach nodded in assent.

"Many would believe she hated her husband enough to want a handsome young man to take the castle - and her."

"And few would believe she hated him enough to kill her own child by him," said Ailean.

"And it will help keep the respect of my men."

"True. It will be as you say, captain," said Tearlach. And he left to spread the word that the woman was not to be touched. The story would be spread later when the pillaging was done.

For a long time after he left, Ailean continued to look out over the ocean. He did not look down to the rocks below. He simply stood, quietly, enjoying his revenge.

Then he spoke softly to himself.

"Ahhhh, Tearlach, my friend, in many ways you are still too soft. And the story you will tell is so much closer to truth than you will ever know."

Chapter Twenty

Consolidation

Eachann wasn't sure what to think.

Clearly his brother had something in mind when he took Mingarry. The castle held a strategic place overlooking the Sound of Mull and the Loch Sunart. There was a place for him to moor his ships that was defensible. The castle was not in great shape, but it was serviceable.

The lands nearby were rich and fertile, though they would take some tending.

At this thought Eachann smiled. If he took no action, then his brother would be forced to spend time managing two widely separate estates. And as Eachann had learned, first by helping his father and later by doing it himself, the care of a castle and the surrounding lands was a full-time job.

"And a job that will keep my younger brother too busy to go pirating the shipping lanes so close to Mull."

* * *

Tearlach looked at the castle and despaired. It was an old structure and while it had a commanding view, it was in need of massive repair. So much that he doubted Ailean was even aware of the expense involved.

Ailean smiled next to him.

"Place looks like dung, doesn't it?"

"You reading minds now?" laughed Tearlach.

"It's obvious. You look at the walls and you scowl. Your face twists up like a child tasting fish liver oil."

Ailean smiled.

"We don't have to rebuild the place. Just fortify it a bit."

"Well even fortifying it will take a lot of work."

"We have a number of able-bodied men and you can recruit more workers from the village we now control.

"That's true, but most of those people will be hard pressed to provide for the winter with so many men gone."

Ailean shrugged.

They'll survive. They may have to cluster together and share to survive, but they will keep going. These are people of the land. They don't know how to do anything else but toil and work. If they don't survive, we will bring in others who will."

Tearlach was struck by this colder attitude from his friend. Was this something that was new, or was Ailean just revealing an even darker side of himself?

But Ailean was going on and Tearlach shifted his attention back to his friend.

"The lands here will provide for the men I leave behind."

"You're splitting your forces?"

"Yes, I want to lower people's guard. By splitting into two groups and working on the lands I'll give the impression I'm thinking of leaving the pirate life."

"Why?"

"Because I want my next strike to be a surprise. I am going to repay two debts and twist the nose of the Earl for good measure."

"More revenge?"

Ailean eyebrows went up.

"Of course."

"When will it stop?" asked Tearlach, but he already knew the answer.

When they are all humiliated as I was - or dead."

His smile no longer reached his eyes.

"Maybe both."

Chapter Twenty-One

Heartless

The note attached to the body said it all.

"I feel the death of my father.
Now you feel the death of your son.
Seems fitting.
                    - Ailean MacLean"

The still body of John MacLean lay on a makeshift stretcher. The face was cold and grey, twisted in agony, the eyes frozen open. The center of his chest was missing where his heart had been cut out.

The Chief MacLean of Lochbuie looked down at the broken body of his son.

Then up at the retainers who had brought it in. They were battered and wounded, with crudely made bandages still leaking blood in some cases.

"Who did this?" said the Chief. His voice cracked slightly as he tried to maintain rigid control.

One of the men, swallowed and spoke.

"It was Nan Sop. He did this. His men invaded Lochbuie in a half dozen birlinns in the early morning hours. They forged inland making for a local village.

"John met him with a medium sized force thinking he was a simple raider and easily driven off. Your son split his men to try and trap them between the two groups. But his group was struck by the raiders before help could arrive. By the time he realized his error, his men were backed against the cliff wall and surrounded."

The Chief sighed wearily.

"Continue."

"He challenged Nan Sop to honorable combat, a duel."

The Chief nodded, his eyes never leaving the body in front of him.

"What was the reply?"

The man hesitated, then spoke.

"You slandered me in my own house when I could not challenge you. Why should I give you the honor of a fair fight?"

"Then he turned to his men and said, "Kill them all. But bring me young John, I have a message for his father and the Earl of Argyll.""

The Chief's eyes looked up from the body.

"How are you alive to tell this tale?"

"We were in the second group. We tried to reach him but were held at bay. There were nearly eighty men."

He gulped.

"They toyed with us. They could have slain us all, but instead they just pushed us back. If any got too close, they were cut or knocked back by linked shields."

"Nan Sop seemed to be enjoying the whole thing. He was laughing and making jests."

"I - I think he deliberately let us get close so we could hear the screams."

He gulped.

"After they were... done... they drove us away like sheep. We were fewer than ten by then, none without wounds. We lost the rest trying to stop their push toward the village, but Nan Sop swerved when there were only these men left and took his men back to the sea. I circled back with these few who survived to retrieve your son's body."

"I see."

The Chief straightened.

"Leave me."

The men turned and left their Chief to his grief.

Outside the room when the door closed, one of them whispered to the speaker.

He never asked about the heart."

The speaker nodded.

"Aye, and it's better he never finds out what was done with it."

Photo 5 - MacLean of Lochbuie's Castle, Moy Castle

Chapter Twenty-Two

Handfasting

Eachann spoke quietly, persuasively, to his brother.

"We sometimes disagree. But I am serious. You need to wed, or at least handfast with some woman."

Ailean looked at him in disbelief.

"Why would I want to do that? I have little interest in women since Mary. And, I can always get what I want. Mingarry proved that."

"So, the rumors are true!" thought Eachann. *"He did seduce her!"*

"I should be upset that I introduced you two to each other."

Ailean smiled.

"We met long before that, brother. But I admit you did formalize the acquaintance."

Ailean's face was friendly and slightly mocking.

"You obviously have someone in mind."

"Ok." Eachann thought. *"Time to play the game."*

His voice dropped, became intense, concerned.

"Others don't know you Ailean, not like I do."

A smile creased the edges of his lips.

"We are brothers and we need to watch out for each other's interests. A handfasting now will make others believe you are thinking of settling down, of raising a family, of changing your ways."

"I know you are still seeking revenge and I can point you to certain parties who were acting behind the scenes."

He paused as if thinking.

"Not just the wrong at Edinburgh, but at Duart..., and at Cairnburg..."

He saw Ailean's right hand clench and knew the game was his.

"You are stretched thin right now. You are vulnerable. This will make those who want you out of the way hesitate."

The intensity of his voice grew.

"They are sheep, always wanting to believe that good will come in time."

He laughed harshly.

"We know better."

He leaned forward.

"And they will learn their folly in time - and, as always, too late."

He winked at Ailean.

"A wolf with a litter is still a wolf."

They both laughed.

* * *

"Why her? Of all the women in the Isles did it have to be her?"

Tearlach slammed his axe into the tree so hard that the shock sent waves of pain up his arms. He ignored them.

Ailean was his friend. He had never said anything about his interest in Anne of Treshnish. He had spent many lonely nights dreaming of the time he could return to her. And now, after all these years, she was to handfast with his best friend!

He wrenched the axe out of the wood and slammed it into the tree again with brutal force. His hands throbbed.

"What trickster god has decided to plague me?" he wondered.

154

* * *

Eachann watched the handfasting feast with delight. He was especially pleased to see the sour look on Tearlach's face. The man had spoiled many of Eachann's plans for Ailean with his interference and it was time for a subtle revenge. He remembered Tearlach's casual remark from years earlier. He watched when Anne and Tearlach were in the same room. How he spoke, how he moved, how he watched. He soon confirmed that Tearlach carried a torch and that Anne appeared to be unaware of it. With one stroke, Eachann put out that torch and shoved the ashes in Tearlach's face.

"Every day he will be forced to watch as the woman he loves comes out of his best friend's bedroom. He knows Ailean doesn't love her and it is a marriage of politics and not love."

Eachann savored the feast that followed, eating and drinking his fill. He noted that Tearlach ate almost nothing.

* * *

Anne was pleasantly surprised as she

lay beside the man she had taken to her bed the night before.

To be sure, Ailean was a good-looking man and she, while attractive, was no beauty.

She had heard of the incident with Mary MacNeil - everyone had. This handfasting was more than a matter of convenience. The MacLean line was thinning, and it was not impossible that the brash young man lying next to her might find himself the possessor of the Clan Chieftainship and all the lands that went with it.

Ailean was capable. He was ruthless when crossed.

These were all things she considered before agreeing to his proposal.

She had gone to their bedding with trepidation.

Her surprise was at his naiveté. He was a bit clumsy, but surprisingly gentle for a man with such a hard reputation. She had expected something just short of rape in his arms. Instead, he had been concerned and thoughtful.

She rolled over carefully so as not to wake him.

This was a side of Ailean she had not expected. He was clearly a complex man.

Warlike, brutal, but honorable in his own way.

"Why me?" she thought.

He clearly had picked her out. She had not pursued him. What was he thinking?

She stretched herself out and moved languorously over next to him.

"Yes, he is a very good-looking man and I know what will please him..."

"He wants heirs," she decided. "He wants to leave a legacy, to leave a mark."

"Well," she thought, "if he wants children, I know how to make that happen."

Chapter Twenty-Three

Taking Gigha

Eachann said he had news.

Tearlach, Angus, and Ailean had come with two birlinns. Now, seated at a large table and enjoying a moderate feast, Tearlach was waiting for the news to fall. He had come to realize that Eachann's information always came at a price. Usually that price was to send Ailean off on a foray that served Eachann's interests more than Ailean's.

The taking of Mingarry was one such maneuver. It took some time, but Tearlach had heard that the wife of MacIan of Mingarry had been introduced by Eachann. Ailean said they had met earlier, but

Tearlach had his doubts.

Ailean often covered for his brother's machinations. His freebooters had made forays into Knapdale and Isla which only served the interests of Eachann. True, there had been rewards - enough to satisfy Ailean's men. And Ailean could be counted on to go after anyone that his brother said was either involved with the death of Lachlan or was part of his detractors at Cairnburg and Duart.

So, when Eachann started talking Tearlach expected the worst.

He wasn't disappointed.

* * *

Eachann was choosing his words carefully. He was certain that Ailean still had strong feelings for his first love, despite his handfasting with Anne and her current pregnancy.

He wondered how Tearlach was taking it. It must twist the knife that she so readily gave Ailean a child.

He could sense that Ailean was getting impatient. Time to test the waters.

"Sister Mary MacNeil, has been buried on church grounds at Gigha."

He paused.

"I thought you would want to know."

There was total silence in the room.

Ailean's voice, when he broke the silence, held emotions barely being kept in check.

"What happened?"

"It's not clear. There are multiple stories circulating."

He hesitated.

"Some say that the convent where she was staying was run down and the Laird of Gigha refused to maintain it, claiming that it was the church's business. She took a fever from the draft and died from it."

Ailean, nodded, his brow furrowed. When he spoke, his voice was hard.

"You said rumors. That implies more than one..."

"There is a less savory one that the Laird himself took a fancy to her. She spurned him, claiming she belonged to God."

He paused as if looking for a delicate path.

"The Laird of Gigha refused to take 'no' for an answer."

He paused a beat.

"Then, to hide his foul deed, he had her poisoned."

The cup in Ailean's had shattered,

spilling ale across the table.

No one moved.

Ailean's face was beet red. His breath was labored.

Tearlach thought Ailean might run from the room straight to his ship and sail to Gigha without thought to the consequences.

"I need to calm him down."

Tearlach spoke.

"How much truth to this rumor do we have? Do any of the tellers of this tale also claim to be witnesses?"

Eachann sat back and opened his arms out, palms up.

"It is a rumor. Coming to me by indirect means. I have received no direct report. I was able to confirm she has died, and even that the convent is in disrepair, but as to the cause of her death, nothing can be confirmed..."

He took a drink of ale.

"Although," he added, "I am still trying to find out."

He looked into his cup to see how much was left and motioned for a servant to fill it. When the servant had finished filling his cup, he added...

"Gigha is not being very forthcoming about the matter."

Eachann looked over at Ailean.

"I'm sorry to be the bearer of such tidings."

"Liar," thought Tearlach. *"You want control of Gigha and Ailean will move heaven and earth to get it for you."*

Ailean rose.

"I'm sorry brother, but I find this news has spoiled my appetite. If you will excuse me..."

Eachann nodded.

"Of course, brother, please go do whatever will bring you solace."

Tearlach sat in amazement.

"I would expect him to choke on such words!" he thought.

Ailean turned and left. When he had cleared the hallway, Eachann turned to Tearlach.

"Go with him. We both know what he will do if you do not slow him down. Make him see that one ship will not take Gigha."

Tearlach sat his own face turning a slow burning red.

"How could you bait your own brother like that?" was on his lips.

Eachann held up a hand to forestall what Tearlach was about to say.

"I know what you are thinking and if you say those words, I would have you put to death before sunrise."

Tearlach glared but checked his tongue.

Eachann shook his head reprovingly.

"You think yourself cool headed, but you are not," said Eachann.

He slapped the table so hard the dishes jumped.

"You think that I did this to maneuver him to my will. Think deeper."

Eachann paused to let Tearlach cool, then spoke.

"If I did not tell my brother, he would have heard in another way, at another time, where I could not act in his best interests."

Eachann sighed.

"Here, you can counsel him. I cannot. You can get him to plan his revenge. I know he will take it, and I will do nothing to prevent it. You have my word as Chief of the MacLeans. The repercussions will fall on me. I will bear them."

"Go now. Save your friend from his temper."

Eachann turned to Angus who had sat quietly near the end of the table the entire time.

"You should ready sail, I expect Ailean will want ships from Torloisk as well as Mingarry. There will be blood spilled on both sides and I expect there will be more plunder than usual. Ailean will not care much who dies."

Tearlach nodded at Angus.

Both men rose and left the table.

Tearlach paused and looked back from the doorway at Eachann. On his face was a cautious look of respect. He nodded once and was gone.

* * *

The two men left, and Eachann sat back and smiled. It had gone exactly as planned. Eachann would see Gigha come into MacLean hands and Tearlach's suspicions would be allayed for a time.

"I send a sword at Gigha rather than a club," he thought.

He drank fresh ale, pleased at his own creativity.

"Tearlach can be as useful as Ailean," he mused.

And as he signaled for more meat, he smiled.

"Smart men can be much more easily led when they draw their own conclusions for you."

* * *

Ailean's ships landed on the northern coast out of sight of the fortress around Gigha. His men had been moving south carefully, preparing for the assault, for two days. They made ladders and prepared burning torches to throw.

In the early morning hours Angus and a birlinn had sailed past Gigha and made to land at the southern part of the island. That would draw a party of men out of the area and leave the rest more vulnerable. Angus's men were to leave as soon as the opposing party arrived and sail back to join the main group for the assault. With a fair wind, they could beat their pursuer's back.

* * *

Ailean stood arrayed for battle, shield and axe in hand.

His voice was careful with a fey tone that said how close to his berserker ancestors he now was. Men saw the look on his face and in his eyes. And they prayed that they were not between him and anyone he was going after. Ailean's voice was raw as he spoke.

"Today, I wear no helm. I want the Laird of Gigha to see the face of the vengeance that comes for him this day!"

He raised his axe.

"I want him to know that all the angels in heaven and all demons of hell will not stop my vengeance this day."

Angus and Tearlach stood behind him. Both were in full battle gear. Tearlach wore his hauberk. Their faces were grim. Men used to slaughter, shifted uneasily. No one spoke.

Ailean's head turned. His eyes caught the eyes of men used to seeing death. The coldness in his face was terrifying.

"These are my orders. Follow them."

He did not raise his voice. He did not need to.

"Touch none of the nuns or priests! They are to be unharmed!"

For just a moment his voice turned so soft only Tearlach heard.

"For she loved them all."

Then his voice boomed out.

There will be no sanctuary for any who flee to the church or any other place."

He drew a thumb across the blade of his axe. A thin line of blood ran down the blade. He had been sharpening it for hours.

Almost a hundred and twenty men stood to listen to his words.

"I will have the head of the Laird of Gigha on a spear by the end of this day! It will hang from the highest rampart! I will have no man, woman, or child of his family left alive to the youngest babe. I will burn his home, his farms, and his barns. I will slaughter his cattle and leave them to rot in the fields. I will pour saltwater on his fields and I will pee on his father's grave."

At this one of his men laughed.

Ailean looked left towards the man and the laughter silenced instantly.

He looked back to the center of the group.

"Take whatever plunder you desire from Gigha - food, drink, treasure… women. But touch nothing that belongs to the church.

He looked carefully at his men.

"Nothing."

Tearlach spoke up.

"It will be as you wish, captain."

He raised his axe above his head. Blood ran down the blade.

"Today I am Laird of Torloisk! Tonight, I will be Laird of Torloisk and Gigha!"

* * *

The wind favored his ships. He swept

around the island with seven boats and raced down the coast towards the estate and tower at Gigha. He could see in the distance that Angus's ship was already tacking back towards him.

The men who had chased off to rout Angus would likely beat them back to the tower, but they would be tired from the trip down and back. They would have little time to prepare for the real assault. His own men in the woods would slow their advance by firing the fields nearby.

When Ailean landed the men of Gigha were in disarray.

The assault on the estate and the tower that watched from the hilltop caused many casualties on both sides. Men died climbing the ladders; men died defending the outer walls; men died trying, in vain, to put out fires; men died in the woods; Ailean fired the sides of the tower using smoke and heat to kill those within. A crude battering ram opened the doors of the main house and it was there that the Laird of Gigha died.

He and his men fought, no quarter asked, and none given.

Ailean did not say a single word throughout the battle.

When the Laird and all his men had

fallen, Ailean emerged with a head on a spear. His men forced the tower and he climbed up through the smoking ruins to place the bloody trophy on the highest part of the tower wall.

He descended to ragged cheers and his men scattered to claim their spoils.

Tearlach stayed near Ailean as he searched through the graveyard, until he found a particular grave.

When he found it, Tearlach moved to the edge of the graveyard and let none approach so Ailean could mourn.

If his men heard the awful wail he gave, none ever said a word.

All his men said that the redness of his eyes was from the smoke of the climb in the tower.

However, they all knew better.

* * *

Eachann was incensed.

"He did what?"

The man shuffled his feet and spoke in a soft voice.

"He has claimed the island and stationed three of his birlinns there."

Eachann sat back and banged his fist on the chair in frustration.

He had thought that Ailean would take the island, kill most of the inhabitants, and burn most of the buildings. Then he would mourn for a day or two and take his fleet back to Mingarry. Eachann would then send men to reclaim the island for the MacLeans.

"What is he doing?" he asked.

The spy relaxed now that Eachann was clearly gathering facts.

"He has men working day and night fixing up the church and the convent."

"What about the village?"

"The men were too busy chasing for loot and women to burn much and the buildings were spaced. A late evening downpour dampened men's mood.

In the morning, Ailean had many of the villagers rounded up from the forest where they fled.

Then he declared himself Laird of Gigha and made them swear fealty or die."

The spy paused.

He gathered his pirates and he told them that they would claim the whole isle and defend it. He sent two birlinns. One to bring workers from Mingarry and the other to bring workers from Torloisk. They should be back by now."

"So, he means to keep Torloisk,

Mingarry, and Gigha!" thought Eachann.

"My brother grows ambitious," his voice rumbled.

Then another thought struck him.

"Of course! She is buried there."

He cursed his own foolishness.

"He would give up Torloisk and Mingarry before he would be parted from Gigha, now," he muttered.

Turning the issue over in his mind he tried to look at how this could still be turned to his advantage.

"Ailean still has a problem," he mused. *"He is stretched thin."*

He swirled his glass ignoring the ale that spilled on the table.

"How is he able to hold so much land?" He wondered. *"Why don't his men revolt?"*

"Tearlach," he decided. *"Tearlach is smart and loyal. And I suspect Anne is having a hand in keeping the locals in line."*

Eachann sat back and smiled.

"This game goes to you, brother," he conceded.

Chapter Twenty-Four

Eachann Plans

Eachann sat on the large chair he liked to use when thinking. In his hand he held a large mug of ale. Word had reached him that Sir John Campbell, the murderer of his father, had appealed to the council on behalf of the Earl of Argyll for the grant of extraordinary powers to "restore peace to the country."

Eachann smiled grimly. It was an admission that the Campbells were losing in the feud between them.

"The alliance with the MacDonald's was worth it," he decided. Together, they had ravaged Roseneath and Craignish. The Campbells had retaliated of course,

attacking Tiree and Mull as well as plundering parts of Movern.

"I doubt they will mention that in their accounts of 'seeking peace'," he thought.

"My brother has done quite a bit to annoy them as well and I'm sure he would like nothing better than to get his hands on John Campbell of Cawdor."

He raised his glass and drank slowly.

"As would I," he conceded to himself.

His spies had reported that the council had refused, but did send cannons, powder, and shot to Dumbarton.

"Argyll is up to his tricks again," Hector decided. *"The council knows he was behind the murder of my father. And the King is embarrassed that he didn't protect him when he had offered safe passage. Instead he lets John Campbell walk around a free man instead of beheading him for the murderer he is."*

He took another drink.

"Now the King wants things quieted down. He's got trouble brewing with King Henry. He wants to get all his subjects behind him in case there's a war - which there will be. Henry's not going to stop And James' taxes are not endearing him to the nobility."

"Perhaps," he thought, *"it is time to*

173

expose the Earl of Argyll as a thief. It's clear that the monies he has been collecting are not going to the crown. But I can't expose him alone. I need to get others to join me."

He smiled.

"And, while I'm at it, let's see what the King of England would offer for the support of the Clan Maclean in his efforts to bring reform to the Scottish Isles."

He began composing letters in his mind.

"One to the clans under Argyll asking for details of their abuse, one to the King passing those details along..."

He finished his drink with a satisfied smile.

"And one to the King of England to see what the Protestant Reformation might bring to the coffers of Clan Maclean."

Chapter Twenty-Five

Unversed in Diplomacy

Eachann was reflecting on his brother's fortunes.

"He sweet talks a pardon from the Crown, and still manages to continue to prey on Scottish holdings."

He ate with less relish than usual.

"Excellent play, brother. Do you now serve Scottish or English interests? Either way, I will have to be even more discreet."

He signaled for more vegetables. The ale was making his stomach sour.

"Yes, Ailean was striking hard at those who had wronged him, while being careful not to draw retribution onto himself."

Thinking about it he realized most of

those who had wronged him on the day he left were dead or had paid their debt in other ways.

"Soon there may be no one left for you to seek vengeance against. That would make you more dangerous and much less controllable."

The vegetables were cold and bitter. He pushed them away.

"I think you need someone new to focus on, brother."

But, before Eachann could come up with a plan to alter Ailean's ambitions, events nearby sent Ailean's on a new course.

* * *

"He said what about me?" Ailean roared.

Tearlach was trying to placate him, but Ailean was incensed.

"This might not end well if he takes off unprepared as he is likely to do," he thought.

Ailean had been drinking with some of his men when word came of the ditty circulating about him. His hair was disheveled, and his shirt was stained where ale had spilled on it. A tray of food had been knocked to one side.

Tearlach tried to make light of it.

"He's not a warrior, Ailean, he's a poet. You know how crazy they can be."

Ailean glared with bloodshot eyes. He had partied heavily with his men after the last successful raid. At another time the words would probably not faze him. But now with a foul stomach and an even fouler mood, Ailean was close to snapping.

"They don't know how crazy I can be."

Ailean turned to Angus.

"Ready the birlinns! I wish to pay a visit to my cousin in Coll!"

He slammed his palm onto the table.

Let's see how well he writes from a dungeon cell in Tarbert!

* * *

It was a combination of surprise and luck that ended with Ailean standing back in Gigha with the poet, Hector MacLean of Coll, before him in chains. His men had struck on a moonless night. Still drunk and disorderly, they caught the guards completely unawares.

It was sheer numbers which carried them into the hall where Hector lived. Hector, to his credit, stood and asked that

177

all be spared since he was the man they wanted. The pirates obliged him by wrapping him in chains and dragging him to a birlinn. Only those who opposed them, were killed. And with so many men on Ailean's side few saw the point in opposition.

Ailean was initially for killing anyone who had listened to the scandalous poem. Tearlach argued that it would just make the poem famous and everyone would seek it out. Ailean relented, seeing the wisdom of Tearlach's advice.

Surprisingly, it was Anne not Tearlach, who asked for the poet's life. And, Ailean granted her the wish though it went against his feelings.

Anne smiled and addressed him.

"It is possible for anyone to change with enough time. It is easy to see the bad in others, much more difficult to see the good."

She nodded towards Hector and said.

"I suspect you should meditate on that for a while."

He was hauled away and placed in a dungeon cell.

* * *

It was six months later when Anne quietly asked that the poet be brought from the dungeon to table.

Ailean was suspicious.

"Why do you want Hector brought here?"

"I have received word from one of his jailors that he has repented his insult to you and wishes to make amends."

Ailean looked at Tearlach, who shrugged.

"I know nothing of this," he said.

Ailean looked dubious.

"And how will he do that?"

"I believe," said Anne, "that he has composed a new poem. One that you would find much more to your liking."

Ailean nodded.

"I see."

Ailean sat for a moment, thinking.

"He is a MacLean, dear." she added, "They do not bend easily."

"Indeed," said Ailean.

He turned his head. "Angus, go to the dungeons and fetch Hector of Coll."

Anne interrupted quietly.

"Please clean him up, dear, I don't want the boys thinking he can come to table smelling like he does now."

John and Hector sat dutifully next to

their mother. They were dressed well and sat up straight as was proper. But it was impossible for Ailean to miss the smirk on their faces as they thought of a smelly old man being brought to the table to apologize.

Tearlach wondered how she knew of his odor but did not ask. He could see that Ailean was having similar thoughts.

Tearlach added, "It's true that people coming from the dungeons rarely smell enticing."

At this, several at the table, including Ailean, laughed.

Ailean shook his head wearily. He knew he was being manipulated, but he suspected that it might be to his long-term advantage.

"Alright then, Angus, make sure he is cleaned up before he comes to apologize."

Then he turned to Anne,

"But if it is not a true apology, he can expect a much longer stay."

Anne bowed her head and nodded. The boys giggled, then straightened their faces at Anne's reproving look.

Ailean winked at the boys, leaving them to wonder if their father was also playing a game of his own.

The night wore on and food and ale was consumed in quantity. Many were laughing wondering what Hector would do to try and win his freedom.

Ailean seemed in a jovial mood, which was unusual for him.

Tearlach watched Anne for any sign of what was to come.

He saw her signal a servant and whisper something.

The servant nodded and left the hall.

Angus returned.

"I had him cleaned up as you ordered. I was going to bring him naked, but since Lady Anne is present, I threw some clothes on him."

Ailean looked over at Anne as several people grinned.

His voice was casual as he said, "Unusually good thinking on your part Angus."

There were several loud guffaws and both Angus and Anne turned red.

Tearlach was surprised.

"They are in this together!" he realized.

Hector appeared.

The pants were too big, and the shirt ballooned around him. The sleeves were too short, and he clomped in oversized boots.

He was a comic sight.

Ailean sat back and grinned.

Hector stood and hung his head.

"The clothes are fitting; I was a buffoon to have insulted you."

"A good beginning," said Ailean.

"In apology for my error in judgment, I have composed a piece which I hope will win your favor."

Ailean nodded.

Tearlach noticed the servant returning with a satchel. It was delivered to Anne who took it gingerly.

It took Tearlach a second to realize what it was.

Anne rose and addressed Ailean.

"If the man wishes to sing for us, he should also provide a melody."

"What do you propose?" said Ailean.

"I heard Hector once as a child, singing for the entertainment of the children of Treshnish. I believe he used one of these..."

From the satchel she drew out a beautiful lute, highly polished, which seemed to glow in the firelight.

Ailean was grinning now.

He winked at Tearlach.

"It seems that Anne has been preparing this request for quite some time," he said dryly.

He looked down at Hector.

"Let's hope your apology is equally thoughtful."

Hector took the instrument gratefully and checked the tuning. He altered one of the strings and strummed a chord. The tone was excellent, and he smiled in pleasure. He took a deep breath and his tone became that of a troubadour.

"I call this piece 'Ailean Maclean's March'"

It was a rousing tune backed by an excellent voice. The lute carried the melody and by the end every person in the room, except Ailean, was cheering.

Ailean was grinning like a child with his favorite candy.

When the song ended, everyone turned to see what Ailean would say.

For a moment he looked at Anne and then turned to Angus.

"Take this man from my sight," he said.

For a moment, there was total silence in the room.

Then Ailean added. "And return him to me when he is clothed as a proper guest should be dressed."

There was an audible sigh in the room.

Ailean had an almost boyish grin on his face as he spoke.

"You have earned your freedom this day, Hector. Your lyrics show the skill with which great poets choose their words. Will you join us for dinner? I believe there is more than enough for a new guest."

Hector nodded, saying nothing. There were tears in his eyes.

"Then you shall join us when you have changed your clothes."

And as Hector turned to leave, Ailean added quietly in a voice that was so cold that even Anne shivered.

"And I hope that, in the future, you will choose all your words about me with equal care."

Photo 6 - Tarbert Castle

Chapter Twenty-Six

Bribes

Tearlach, Angus, and Anne sat with Ailean around a glowing fire. The four were relaxing after a good meal. Ailean had asked Anne to join them, which was a rare occasion.

Tearlach watched as Anne maneuvered to sit comfortably. Her swollen belly was an announcement that yet another MacLean was on the way. Two sons already she had delivered, Hector and John, and now a third!

She turned an amused smile at Tearlach who looked away in embarrassment.

"The midwife says this one will be a girl," she announced.

"Well, if she's right you will finally have someone to help with the wash," said Ailean.

"About time," said Anne, "It's a chore trying to get all the blood out of your clothes!"

At this Ailean laughed and the others joined in.

Ailean's face turned serious. He turned to Angus.

What does the Earl of Argyll offer?" said Ailean.

His emissary says they will grant the lands of Kilcharmaig in Knapdale to you in pursuit of an end to the enmity between us.

So, the Earl seeks an alliance?

"A friendship of sorts," said Tearlach. "I'm sure it will last as long as you are strong and able and command a fleet he respects."

"He was behind the death of my father,"

"That was only a rumor gathered from your brother. Likely though it was," said Anne.

Tearlach nodded.

"He has paid in lives, land, and the court's favor for that mistake." said Tearlach.

"If you continue to make war on the

Earl, the court might take notice," added
Anne.

Ailean sat back and thought for a long
time.

"The land is rich, and we wouldn't
have to plunder it to gain our wealth."

He looked at Angus.

"How do you think the men will
react?"

"Well," said Angus. "We've some new
lads who are a bit restless. The foray to
Mull to get Hector, placated them for a
while. Many are getting older. More than a
few now have wives and families. They are
not so interested in plunder as before."

"What about you, Angus?" said
Ailean.

Angus smiled. "Well, you've never lost
a fight yet, and it's been a long run for a
freebooter. But I guess that if you can get
the spoils without the fight, that's not a bad
thing."

Ailean smiled. "Fair enough. Let me
know if the younger lads get too restless
and we will see if we can find something for
them to do."

Angus nodded.

Ailean smiled at his wife and looked to
Tearlach.

"Tell the emissary that we appreciate

his generous grant of land and accept it with pleasure. Tell him, he has our friendship and will have our future support."

Ailean turned to Angus,

"Tell the men quietly, over ale, that the Earl has paid blood price for my father and his lands and ships are no longer to be molested."

Angus looked confused.

"You do not wish to announce your victory to the men?"

Ailean shook his head.

"No," he said, "If word got back to those in the Courts in Edinburgh, the shaming of the Earl would be too great, and he would be forced to renege and attack us."

Anne murmured softly.

"You really did learn some things at that English Court."

"I let that fat poet go for you, didn't I?" said Ailean.

"Come now," she replied. "The poem was really rather good, and it certainly was flattering."

They all laughed.

When they had stopped, Tearlach cleared his throat.

Ailean looked over.

"I have other news. We have another emissary who has approached us with an offer."

Ailean and Anne both looked surprised.

Angus smiled.

Ailean seemed to know everything that happened within all of Scotland sometimes. For him to be surprised was a feat.

He and Tearlach had pulled off the impossible in his mind.

"Angus and I have met with an emissary from the Chieftain of the MacDonald's. He approached us at sea on his way to Mingarry to make an offer."

Ailean's voice was cold but curious.

"And what does the MacDonald want of a pirate?"

Tearlach smiled.

"He wishes to press his claim as Lord of the Isles."

Ailean frowned.

"That kind of support could bring me the Scottish Court's disfavor and jeopardize any pact with the Earl of Argyll. What could he possibly offer me to make such a risk worthwhile?"

Tearlach's face was impassive but Ailean could see just a hint of a smile creasing the edges.

"Tarbert Castle."

Angus laughed.

"You already possess Tarbert! It was a grand expedition capturing it! We have held it for nearly two years now! What is MacDonald thinking, offering you what is already yours?"

Ailean nodded.

"He is offering me peaceful a transition. As long as Tarbert and the surrounding lands are contested I have to prepare a defense against a MacDonald assault. He is offering an alliance where no lands change hands except on paper, but both sides gain. He gives up that which he no longer controls and gains my alliance and a promise of no further incursions on his lands. I keep what I have taken and need not fear him attempting to retake what I have captured.

He paused.

"Also, the MacDonald's fought with my brother against the Campbell's. They both sought redress for grievances. They took some blows as a result but kept to their word."

He smiled. "It's brilliant."

He nodded to himself.

"I think I might like this man."

Chapter Twenty-Seven

Eachann Becomes a Guest

Ailean slammed the table with his fist so hard that plates jumped up and fell to the floor. A candelabra fell over and a servant righted it quickly, picking up candles that popped loose and replacing them. In her haste, Tearlach noticed that she ignored the hot wax that streamed over her fingers. Servants hesitated and then ran to pick up the mess taking care not to look at Ailean or any of the others present in the room.

What do you mean, "My brother has been taken by the king?"

Angus looked uncomfortable.

"Word is going around that King

James is visiting the Isles in command of a great fleet. He has been visiting the chieftains and taking them, one by one as hostages."

"Why?"

There was a coldness in Ailean's voice that Tearlach had come to recognize. People were going to die.

Angus shifted a bit from one foot to the other.

"It's to make you stop," he said bluntly.

"Not just you," he hastened to add. "It's to stop the Clans from fighting with each other."

"The King has issued an edict that makes the Chieftain of each clan responsible for the actions of all members under that clan."

"He wants to stop you from plundering. He's holding your brother as hostage for your good behavior."

For a long time Ailean sat quietly.

Tearlach watched his friend closely for any signs of what he was thinking.

"I see," said Ailean. "Word has reached James of my visit to the King of England."

He looked around the room and men looked nervously at each other. His smile was slow in coming.

"It was inevitable. Argyll offers me a bribe on one side and tries to take Duart with the other."

He looked thoughtful.

"Argyll has a grievance against Eachann for his disgrace and imprisonment as well. My brother wrote his letter of appeal to the king a little too well. He had far too much evidence for the King to ignore it. As a result, Argyll has been stripped of his title and much of his influence. In consequence, he has struck out at all of those who were included in the letter. Word is, he has embraced King Henry although I suspect King James is still unaware of that."

Ailean gestured to a servant for ale. It was hastily poured. Ailean tasted then settled back in his chair.

"James grows increasingly erratic. His vengeance on his father, Angus, and the Douglas Clan went too far when he seized Douglas lands and burned Lady Glamis as a witch. She was well liked and innocent. Everyone knew it. It set many of the Clans wondering if their lands would be next. His taxes are disliked, and he has even risked papal displeasure by taxing church lands. Finally, he has bouts of illness during which his enemies move against him. They are too well informed."

"It's all politics," he sighed.

"This is not good."

Tearlach asked the question all were wondering.

"What will you do?"

Ailean sat back and motioned for food. A plate was quickly placed before him. He began to eat calmly, then paused as all around him waited. He shrugged as if the next thing to do was obvious.

"Play politics and free my brother, of course."

Chapter Twenty-Eight

Ailean Prepares

It was a side of Ailean that Tearlach had almost forgotten existed.

Ailean struck out on pirating forays that seemed to be almost invisible. His men took ships and cargo with impunity while taking great care to touch no ship that might put his brother in danger.

His men were kept busy.

At the same time Ailean cast out feelers for men who could report to him on the condition of his brother. He was worried when the King's fleet stopped in Dumbarton, but his informants told him that the King had sent the Clan Chiefs on to Edinburgh. Ailean discovered that

James of Islay, the other major rebel petitioner against Argyll, had joined his brother on the journey.

When King James returned to Edinburgh several of the Chiefs were freed in exchange for promises and hostages against their good behavior. Eachann and James of Islay were not. According to his spies, the treatment of the Chiefs was not unduly harsh, but they seethed with rage at the insult of their word not being taken as sufficient in negotiations. Ailean smiled to himself. Perceived insults to a Clan Chief were the source of most of the conflicts plaguing the Isles. James was probably right to lay harsh terms and demand hostages.

However, most of that hostility rebounded to the benefit of the Earl of Argyll in the past. Even now, Argyll, with many of his schemes exposed, and his titles stripped, was still wielding considerable power.

However, Ailean had found a weakness.

The Earl of Glencairn had become the eternal foe of Argyll. And, while Glencairn had little he could do to influence the King, Ailean still marked him as a potential ally.

"The enemy of my enemy..." he

thought.

He secretly sent men to assist in the protection of Duart. His ships patrolled the waters and harried ships that looked suspicious. If the Earl of Argyll thought about attacking Duart in Eachann's absence, his own presence in the waters quashed the idea.

Some of his men quietly questioned his motives.

He spelled it out for them over a bout of drinking after a particularly good raid into Irish territory.

"We bide our time and keep our axes sharp. Soon the Chiefs of Maclean and MacDonald will be returned. And when that happens there will be conflict. Argyll will be the target."

"Why do we care?" said one younger sailor.

"Argyll has been a thorn in my side for far too long. But, most importantly, he has bled the Isles of riches. Under attack from the Macleans and the MacDonalds, his lands will be available to plunder. His ships will be undermanned and heavy with supplies and booty. They will be easy pickings!"

He rubbed his hands together.

"A little patience and a big reward!"

He laughed out loud.

"What we will take from Argyll ships will make this raid look like scrawny leavings."

He lurched to his feet and raised his ale.

"To plunder!"

His men roared in approval as he drained the cup.

He staggered out of the hall and down towards his rooms, Tearlach beside him.

"Do you think they believed it?" he said straightening and losing all appearance of being inebriated.

"Yes. They think they understand your scheme."

"Good."

Chapter Twenty-Nine

The Chaos Year

The battle of Solway Moss was a disaster. The king was ill, and control of the King's forces was disputed. Amidst the turmoil the English cavalry attacked and, although they were a much smaller force, the Scottish fell into confusion and attempted to retreat and regroup. The retreat turned into a rout and the Scots were trapped by the river and swamp, losing men to both. Many surrendered and the battle turned into a humiliating defeat for the Scottish.

Ailean received word almost as fast as the King. Initially, the losses were greatly exaggerated, but Ailean was much more interested in how he might benefit from the chaos and bickering of the clans over blame for the defeat.

Then came news of the death of King James.

Rumors abounded about his death all of which were ignored by Ailean. A second rumor which he was quick to confirm was that just before his death he became a father again - to a girl.

With no male heirs Ailean could see that the time was coming when he might be able to make a move to rescue his brother.

He followed with interest over the next few days as Mary of Guise was removed as the child's guardian and Cardinal Beaton, declared himself guardian and governor based on a will he claimed he had from the King. Then came word that the Earl of Lennox and the Earl of Argyle were both coming to take the infant - also named Mary - into their custody for her protection by force if necessary.

Ailean could see the chaos building and decided it was time to make his move. If Argyll got to the castle first there was little chance his brother would be alive within a month.

"Angus," he said, "you have many contacts. I'd like for you to use them to send a message to the Earl of Glencairn."

Angus looked surprised. He nodded warily.

"What message do you wish me to give him?"

"Tell him I have a plan to greatly humiliate his 'old friend' the Earl of Argyll. If he is interested, I will meet with him at a place of his choosing to discuss it."

Tearlach was shocked.

"You would throw your life into the hands of the Earl of Glencairn? Think of the prestige he would gain with your capture!"

Ailean smiled.

"I have. But with the Court in turmoil my capture would have little value. Bigger games are being played than catching a pirate - even a notorious one. On the other hand, anything that frustrates Argyll at this point would add to the prestige of Glencairn - especially if I make sure that his hands stay clean.

"Are you planning a miracle?" said Angus.

Ailean laughed.

"No Angus, I'm planning to free all the Chiefs held in Edinburgh."

Angus shook his head.

"Beggin' your pardon, Laird - but you

are planning a miracle."

Ailean laughed for a long time.

Chapter Thirty

Plans in Motion

The meeting place was a small inn outside of Edinburgh castle. There was an open area with seating and men gathered at tables and ate and drank.

It reminded Ailean of a barracks, except it was a bit cleaner.

"We must prevent the Earl of Argyll from reaching the Castle at Edinburgh before the Earl of Lennox. We must do it in such a way that it appears natural so that Lennox does not see my hand in events. If he does, he will surely continue my brother's imprisonment. However, I believe we can divert Argyll without losing a man."

Ailean sat with Angus to his left, who

was watching the crowd for any sign of trouble. Tearlach sat to his right doing the same. Ailean sat with his back to the wall. At the table next to him sat a shadowy figure, a cloak covering his face with his back to the wall as well. Across from the cloaked figure sat a large man. He was obviously in heavy chain mail. He did not move but his eyes and ears strained for any sign of betrayal.

Ailean and the figure were angled so they sat partially facing the wall and their companions, but they could talk quietly to each other without turning if they were careful. Spread in front of Ailean was a map that could clearly be seen from the other table.

Ailean continued, as if talking to his friends in front of him, but the conversation was for the man at the next table.

"The Earl is mustering forces here. His finger touched a place on the map. From this location he can reach the castle well before Lennox. However, if we sail our entire fleet to here - he pointed - and let ourselves be seen from shore, word will swiftly reach Argyll. The Earl will believe that we are planning an attack on his lands. He will move his forces here - he pointed again - and we will simply sail on and take the fleet further up to this point where we already have control.

He smiled.

The Earl will spend at least a day moving his troops in the opposite direction of Edinburgh and another searching for an attack that is never going to come. He will reluctantly turn his forces back to Edinburgh, probably leaving a substantial force behind to contend with a possible pirate strike. However, by that time the Earls of Huntly and Lennox will have arrived first and Argyll's chances to gain entrance to the dungeons will be thwarted.

"I see, said a soft voice. "But I do not see much advantage in this for - my employer - and little embarrassment to Argyll."

Ailean smiled. "The key to his embarrassment will not be my minor diversion. The key will be your employer's insistence to the new Governor that the Chiefs must be freed immediately in order to stabilize the country after the death of the king."

"Once the Chiefs know that Argyll was on his way to Edinburgh with a force, they will see what he planned. They will rally their own forces and begin to harry him from all sides.

"You have heard of the Will that Cardinal Beaton claims is from the king?"

The shadowy figure nodded.

"It is a forgery, no doubt, meant to give him control and keep Henry from bringing the reformers into Scotland. "

"It may indeed be a forgery, but I suspect King Henry's designs are much larger than that, now that King James is gone," said Ailean.

The figure nodded again.

"If Henry moves, you will need the support of all the clans to keep Scotland from becoming a vassal to England," said Ailean. "This is the lever to move the Earl of Lennox to our thinking."

The figure nodded.

"If several of the Chiefs are still in Edinburgh when Henry moves, it may be too late to do anything."

The glass of ale rose and fell quietly.

"There is still the problem of getting the Chiefs away from Edinburgh and back to their own territories."

Ailean took a sip from his own mug.

"If you could persuade the governor to release them, making it public the day after they are actually released, I could provide a few small fast ships to pick them up and spirit them away. Once they are free of

Edinburgh and back to their clans, I am sure that the 'embarrassment' of Argyll will begin very quickly."

Ailean heard a low chuckle from the shadowy figure.

"I will convey your proposal to my - employer. I'm sure he will accept. When do you plan to move?"

Ailean smiled.

"The ships will divert Argyll's troops in three days' time. Once Lennox arrives in Edinburgh your - employer - must move quickly. Cardinal Beaton will be removed as Governor and Regent. In fact, he will probably be arrested and thrown in the dungeons. Lennox will likely take his place as governor. Then you must persuade him to release the Chiefs. He will see it as a chance to win favor with the Clans and help cement his Governorship. Done quickly, before Argyll arrives, and the Earl will be embarrassed in court and find his fall and winter filled with troubled sleep."

"And to effect the escape of the Chiefs?"

"Hang a Glencairn standard from any window or battlement that faces the sea on the morning that they are to be freed. That evening, my men will come to the base of the castle and escort the Chiefs away."

"How will I know the ships?"

"You won't. One man will approach the gate and show you this…"

He held up a small bright dagger, turning it over, as if examining if for flaws. Then, as if satisfied, he put it away.

"Once the Chiefs are away your employer's part of the affair is concluded. He can be miles away when the announcement of the release is made."

"Oh, he won't go too far away. I'm sure he will want to see the face of the Earl of Argyll when he realizes that all the Chiefs, he persuaded King James to hold here, have gone home to their clans."

The dark figure placed a mug of ale on the table and rose.

"Good ale," he said aloud. Tearlach and Angus stiffened. Several men around the room rose quietly and began to leave. The figure brushed past the table. Ailean saw a signet ring on the man's hand.

The voice was soft.

"I should have sent an emissary, but I really wanted to meet you. You are as cunning as the rumors say. I have much to do in the next few days, but I will be ready."

Ailean nodded to the back of the departing figure and contentedly drank his ale.

Chapter Thirty-One

Plans Within Plans

"That was close," said Angus. "I was sure we hadn't brought enough men."

"Not really," said Ailean. "I was confident, but I also made additional provisions."

Ailean looked over at Tearlach.

You and I will need to select a group of men to go gather the Chiefs when the time comes. Make sure they are all MacLeans, loyal and trustworthy.

"Why just MacLeans?"

"Our priority is my brother. However, if we involve additional clans in the rescue, we risk old rivalries breaking out at the wrong time."

He turned to Angus.

"The merchant cogs have aroused no suspicion?"

"None," said Angus with a big smile. "We have all the cogs in port and slowly unloading cargo and reloading supplies."

"Excellent! And the crews are arranged as I ordered."

"Yes, each cog is manned by people who are loyal to one of the Clan Chiefs still being held. We put groups together who are allied to minimize the chance of a dispute."

"There have been no incidents?"

"Just one. I took care of it personally," said Angus.

"Mouthy youngster," he added. "Never liked him."

"And the body?"

"It's divided among several pickle brine barrels on the docks. I nailed the skull to the keel of the ship he was on as a warning."

Ailean nodded.

"That should take care of it."

Angus smiled at Ailean.

"It's a noble thing you are doing, trying to free your brother," said Angus.

Ailean put down his mug slowly. His face was no longer grinning.

"Is that what you think?" He shook his head slowly. "Are any of the other men thinking the same?"

"A few," Angus admitted.

Ailean sighed.

"Why would I want to free the Chief of the MacLeans when I would become the Chief of the MacLeans if I let Argyll kill him?"

Angus opened his mouth to speak, but Ailean held up his hand.

"If I let Argyll murder the Chief of the MacLeans, he will next lay siege to Duart. The king is dead, and the council is ineffective. He can move with impunity. He will kill all of Eachann's children and marry his wife to lay claim to the lands. She won't last more than a few months before an 'illness' takes her. Then he will come for me."

He shook his head.

"Within a year, two at most, there wouldn't be a noble MacLean left alive. And he would seize Duart and all the MacLean lands - including those I now hold."

He looked up and signaled the man behind the bar. The man nodded and soon a second mug of ale was brought. Ailean indicated he should wait.

"I could not rally the MacLeans as my

brother can," said Ailean. "They will not flock to my banner."

He pulled out a large purse of coins and placed it on the table.

"So, I keep him alive, to keep Argyll in check."

He signaled the man to take the coins.

"Your Angus's man?"

He nodded.

"The rest are out back, and no one was harmed as ordered."

"Good. Set the owner and his staff free. Give them this in recompense. Then get all your men out of the back rooms. He hesitated. Then pulled out a smaller purse and added it to the first.

"Tell the owner that the second purse is for the keg of ale the men in the back took."

"But the men haven't taken a keg of ale!"

"But they are going to," Ailean said pointing to his mug. "This is very good. Bring the keg to my cog."

Ailean and Tearlach stood and all remaining men in the bar stood as well. Angus looked around surprised.

Ailean grinned at Angus's open mouth expression.

"I believe I said I made additional

provisions." He gestured at the men in the room. These are MacLeans from Duart. I've been having them come in on ships for the past few months and paid to have them hired to work on the docks and do local fishing. They have been keeping an eye on things for me.

"I've had almost two years to plan this. It will succeed."

He drained the second mug. Then he reached into his belt and added a third purse to the table.

He gave a great belch and grinned.

"Make that two kegs."

Chapter Thirty-Two

Freedom

On January 10th, 1543 Cardinal
Beaton appointed himself Chancellor of
Scotland. By January 27th he was removed
from the court and under "house arrest" in
his own Castle at St. Andrew's. The Earl of
Arran had become the new Governor and
the Earl of Glencairn was among the first to
greet him.

In early February on a dark and
cloudy day a banner of Glencairn was hung
from one of the windows of a room in the
castle. Inquiries brought word that the
banner had been accidentally soiled by a
servant and, fearful of her position, she had
endeavored to wash it and hang it out to

dry surreptitiously. The banner was soon pulled back inside and life went on as normal...

Ailean and Tearlach approached the outskirts of the castle with caution. The Maclean men had spread out in a wide fan to look for ambushes of other surprises but found none.

Ailean and Tearlach waited quietly out of view of the sentries as the hours ticked by.

It was close to one in the morning when the main gate suddenly opened, and a small troop of soldiers emerged from the castle. At their head was a dark cloaked figure.

Tearlach and Ailean, also hooded approached the men carefully.

This was the riskiest part of the plan. Ailean was closer to the castle than his own men, but he strode forward as if he hadn't a worry in the world.

When they reached the other group, Tearlach was surprised to see that it was the Earl of Glencairn at the lead. Behind him were a score of soldiers surrounding a group of men looking about warily.

The Earl turned to the men and spoke.

"You have all been formally released

by order of the Earl of Arran, who hopes this act will improve relations between the Regency and the Clans. You are enjoined from battling each other under penalty of censure by the court. These men will convey you to ships that will take you quietly to your respective clans."

"Isn't that Ailean MacLean?" said one. "Are we being sold into pirate slavery?"

Ailean pointed.

"That man is Eachann MacLean, my brother. He walks among you until we reach the ships as proof of my honest intentions."

Eachann looked a bit surprised but then smiled and held out his hands, open palmed.

"I shall be my brother's bond for a while longer it seems," he said.

The Earl of Glencairn signaled his men and they began to withdraw into the castle. Neither man spoke to the other. But just before entering the castle the Earl turned.

"You are a man of your word, Ailean Maclean."

Ailean nodded.

"Enjoy your revenge Earl," he said, and began to lead the group away from the castle and towards his waiting men.

As they made their way down to the docks, one of the other men spoke up in a low whisper.

"Why are we being released at night?"

"The Earl of Argyll is coming, said Ailean. His spies are already in Edinburgh. If you were simply released, they might strike before you could safely leave."

Heads nodded.

"So, the Earl of Argyll is behind our detainment?" said one man.

"He wants our lands and our wealth. If he can't get it through taxes, he'll get it by less 'polite' means," said another.

At this comment there was a low mutter of agreement.

They made the docks without incident. The Chiefs were greeted by their own clan members and hurried aboard the cogs. Sails were raised and as morning rose the ships drifted out one by one.

Maclean men manned one swift birlinn that would ferry Eachann back to Duart. It had a full crew and would sail with a favorable wind.

On the dock, they had a chance to speak alone.

"Are there spies from Argyll in Edinburgh?"

Ailean shrugged. "Probably."

"You stirred the Chiefs up against Argyll."

Ailean said nothing.

"Why did you get me freed?"

"Glencairn did that, not me."

Eachann snorted.

"He does have a grudge against Argyll," he admitted. "But I think he had some inspiration."

"Perhaps."

Eachann smiled.

"So, I ask again. Why?"

Ailean turned and began to walk away towards his own birlinn.

"Self-interest," he called over his shoulder.

"I see," said Eachann.

And he turned and walked thoughtfully to his own ship for the voyage home.

Chapter Thirty-Three

Raid on Bute

The raid was nearly a disaster.

Ailean had set out with two birlinns for a quick foray with Angus and some of the younger men. As he explained to Tearlach, the raid would blood the younger men and get them some beef for the winter.

Recently Ailean had taken a number of men from other lands including some from Ireland and Wales as freebooters. He wanted to see them fight.

Ailean had expected little resistance. He even took his friend, Murdoch Gearr along with him, although Murdoch was not really a fighting man.

Tearlach fretted that he was treating the entire expedition like a lark. It did not help when Tearlach was ordered to stay and watch over Tarbert until Ailean returned.

October was not the best of months to sail. The waters could be choppy and the sea would chill a man in minutes.

Ailean ignored it all and set off in a fine mood.

His jovial mood had evaporated by the time they returned.

The men were tired, weary, and several were wounded. There were several spaces at the oars in both ships.

Tearlach went down to the ships.

Ailean was uninjured and surprisingly so was Murdoch. Ailean's shield was battered and his axe was chipped.

Angus got off the boat first and whispered to Tearlach.

"He's in a foul mood.

The surprise was on us. The Tacksman was on us almost before we got off the boats with a good number of men.

There was a pitched fight, and we lost several lads before we drove them off."

Tearlach was worried.

"How did the Tacksman know you were coming?"

"I've no idea. Maybe someone got lucky and spotted us early. If he had picked a better choice of ground to battle us, it might have gone differently, but Ailean knows how to fight on almost any kind of land.

The Tacksman seemed to make a good choice of higher ground, settling his men across two hills. But Ailean saw the weakness in the choice of terrain and drove straight towards it. He broke the Tacksman's line and split his men in two. Then he turned on one side with the majority of his men driving them off the ridge while a small group held off the rest forcing them to battle up the very hills they had picked! Turned the sheriff's own choice against him.

The battle turned in our favor and the sheriff's men ran. We cut down several and turned it into a rout. Then, before the Tacksman could reorganize his men we gathered the cattle and loaded them onto the ships.

We sailed away just as he returned with more men! The Tacksman was beside himself standing on the beach with dozens of men. I even invited them to swim out and join us!

Angus laughed.

"It was a glorious romp! I don't understand why Ailean was so unhappy with it."

Tearlach listened with growing dismay. He knew Ailean's mind and what he must have thought. He sighed and explained.

"Ailean has always been lucky from his first foray. This is the first time that luck has seemed to turn against him. Ailean believes that luck wins more battles than the best plans men make."

Angus nodded.

"He's right."

"And that is why he broods. He worries that luck may be turning against him."

Angus stopped and his face sobered.

"True, I had not thought of that."

Then he smiled.

"But his luck did not desert him entirely."

Tearlach nodded.

"However, he must wonder how much longer it will last...," he thought.

Chapter Thirty-Four

Lordship of the Isles

"Why?"

Tearlach thought that it was the most reasonable question he had ever heard Ailean ask when in an agitated state.

He and his brother had been arguing for hours now.

Ailean wanted to support James MacDonald of Islay in his bid to become Lord of the Isles.

James MacDonald had given him ownership of his current home, the castle at Tarbert, for that support. And Ailean was pressing his case to any who would listen. There were very few who would. Only the MacDonalds and Camerons had rallied to his side. All the rest had said no or were simply not committing.

Eachann sighed.

"Ailean you are loyal to those with whom you have made alliance. That is a good thing, an unusual thing for a man in your line of — work.

He shook his head.

"But James MacDonald will never become the Lord of the Isles, not even with Donald Dubh MacDonald's endorsement."

"You have to see it, Ailean. He won't become Lord of the Isles because the title is meaningless - except to antagonize the Crown. And we are in no position to antagonize the Crown."

He stood and walked around the table to pat his brother on the shoulder. It was the friendliest gesture Tearlach had ever seen between the two.

"A war with Edinburgh would be lost. We do not have the men, the weapons, or the navy it would take to defeat what could be summoned in just a few weeks."

"The castle is too well defended to take, even by surprise. And even if we did take it, ships and men would pour in and would pound our fortresses and estates into the ground from the sea and land."

"You rode in the warship of the Earl of

Lennox over a decade ago. At that time his ship mounted several cannons that could strike at a fortress like Tarbert and damage it.

Now, warships, would pound it into rubble.

I have heard that they are constructing ships with sixty cannons aboard. Sixty! What do you think all your birlinns could do against a ship like that?

What could they do against a fleet of those ships?"

He shook his head sadly.

No, this is not the time to press for the title. I know it. In your heart, you know it. The Chieftains of the Macleans all know it. It has been discussed. The MacLeans of Lochbuie, Coll, Ardgour, Kingerloch, Barra have all said no. MacNeil of Barra, the Mackinnon, and the Macquarrie, have said no. Macleod of Harris and Lewis have said no."

His voice had a finality to it that was unmistakable.

"I have said no."

Eachann looked at Ailean with a look that mixed sympathy and resolve.

"This thing will not come to pass."

He turned and walked back to his place at the table. He stood with his hands on the back of his chair facing Ailean.

"We will not raise arms against the Earl of Arran and the Crown. To think we will, is a vain hope."

Ailean nodded.

"I hoped I might sway you brother, but your words sway me. I will still support James. As you say, I am loyal to my allies, though I have few. But I will not approach you on this matter again."

Eachann inclined slightly.

"Thank you. Will you stay the night?"

Ailean shook his head.

"No, I return to Tarbert and from there I will convey your message to James."

Eachann spoke softly.

"We face a similar problem with Henry. His forces grow and we squabble amongst ourselves."

He sighed.

"James is a good man. A man worth following. Tell him I said that. But this is not the time."

He shook his head.

"I fear there may never be such a time again. Though we are doomed to try."

Tearlach rose to leave with Ailean.

"If you would, say this to James as well."

"Rash action now would only bring

your people to a grim fate. But, if action is not taken, I believe that the Earl will see no issue with men engaging in a frank discussion."

Ailean nodded and left.

Tearlach followed him.

Ailean said nothing until they were outside of Duart heading to their waiting ship.

"'A fool's errand I was on', he said."

Tearlach could hear the bitterness in his words.

"Eachann has already allied most of the Clans against James. And he has already spoken to the Earl of Arran."

Ailean spit on the ground.

"I believe the Earl will see no issue..."

Ailean turned to Tearlach. His face was grim.

"If James tries to raise arms now, or claim his title, there will be an army on his doorstep in a month."

"What will you do?"

"Forget Tarbert. We sail straight to James and tell him what has happened. If he is wise, he will take no further action and lay no claim."

Ailean drove his fist into an open palm.

"This battle was lost before it began! I

can only hope that James can see that."

Ailean and Tearlach climbed aboard the birlinn. Angus was waiting.

"Where do we sail, captain?"

"We make for Islay, Angus. James needs to be warned."

Chapter Thirty-Five

A Parting of Ways

"*You too?*" was all that Ailean could think.

He was stunned. There was no fight, there was no argument. Anne had come in the middle of the day and asked to speak with him privately. When everyone was dismissed. She had announced that she had a religious revelation and was leaving him to go to the nunnery on Iona.

She was dressed in a simple white gown with a cloth tie gathered around her waist. That waist had grown a bit from the time he had first seen her, with the delivery of three children. Her hips had increased as well, but she carried herself as she always had with a determination that he had admired. Ailean thought she had actually become better looking.

"Now she wants to run away, too."

He was hurt and angry, but her peaceful demeanor sapped the anger from him like a sponge, leaving him quiet and exhausted.

Her words were calm and measured.

"The children are grown, and I feel my time is approaching. I go to make my peace with God. You should too, although I do not think you are quite ready for that."

"Why should I make my peace with God? When did we go to war?"

Anne did not rise to the bait. Instead she just smiled and answered.

"You have never been at war with God, Ailean," she said. "But you have always been at war with yourself."

* * *

In the end she left with a small retinue. John and Hector said goodbye, electing to remain at Tarbert Castle which she expected. Tearlach walked with her to the ship. Angus would convey her to Iona. Tearlach wanted to go but felt it would betray Ailean to leave him now.

231

"In the mood he will be in for the next few weeks it will be a miracle if he doesn't decide to plunder a castle on his own."

Before she left, she pressed a sealed letter into Tearlach's hands.

"After I am gone for a bit, give this to Ailean. He may decide to read it - if enough time has passed."

She smiled.

"I suspect if you gave it to him now, he might toss it in the fire unopened.

Tearlach smiled back.

"She does know him well," he thought.

Tearlach helped her board the ship, touching her for one of the few times in his life. He memorized the feel of her skin and the smell of her in those moments.

"Thank you," she said when she was aboard.

He nodded and was careful to say nothing. He was afraid his voice would crack. He feared he would never see her again and he tried to memorize every line in those few moments.

She smiled and brushed away a lock of blonde hair.

"Be well, Tearlach," were her parting words.

He treasured them.

* * *

From the battlements of Tarbert, Ailean watched as the ship sailed away. He had not gone to the ship to say goodbye. There was an emptiness in him that he could not find a way to fill. His arms and back ached in a way that they had not in his younger days. The weight of years felt like it was pressing in. He would admit to no one how he felt in that moment and none saw. But tears ran freely down his cheeks and he did not try to stop them.

Chapter Thirty-Six

Black Saturday

"How many Scots were killed?"
Ailean's voice was rising slowly in disbelief.

"The reports vary widely but somewhere between six and fifteen thousand."

"And how many Englishmen died?"

"Some say two hundred; some say six..."

"Hundred?"

"Yes, Laird."

Ailean leaned back and rested his arms on his favorite chair.

"Are you sure of this?"

"Yes, Laird. James Hamilton, the Earl of Arran, and Archibald Douglas, the Earl of

Angus, were in command of Queen Mary's forces. The Earl of Arran was acting as her regent in commanding the forces."

"And where was King Henry of England?"

"He was in Europe..."

"He wasn't even at this, this massacre?"

"No, Laird, the English forces were commanded by Edward, the Duke of Somerset."

Ailean sat for a moment.

"My brother was right. We aren't in a position to fight England and we we're doomed to do it anyway."

"So, did the Earl of Angus and the Earl of Arran have the good grace to get themselves killed in the battle?"

"No, Laird. Both earls survived, although I heard over two thousand prisoners were taken."

Ailean shook his head.

"So, in addition to losing a major portion of the male population of the Isles, the English will now be able to ransom the wealth of the Isles to buy back the sons and fathers who are left."

The messenger said nothing, waiting.

Ailean's voice dropped to a growl.

"Was my brother involved in this

fiasco?"

"No, Laird."

He sighed.

"What did they do when they captured Edinburgh? Was Queen Mary taken?"

"They didn't, Laird. Edinburgh did not fall."

"You mean to tell me that, after such a victory, they did not press on to the capital?"

"No, Laird. Somerset withdrew."

"The numbers must have been exaggerated then. The higher numbers are wrong on the Scottish side and the lower numbers are wrong on the English. Say, seven thousand Scotsmen and six hundred Englishmen. Still a disaster, but not so great that a guaranteed route to the castle was opened."

"This news will require thought," he said.

He did not have to dismiss the messenger. He practically fled the room.

Ailean sat for a long time thinking about the size of his own fleet and the size of English warships.

"They will be looking for raiders," he decided.

"English warships could strike at Tarbert, or Gigha, or Mingarry with

impunity."

"This is no time for a foray and my men will have to be kept busy. Otherwise, there could be trouble."

He signaled a nearby guard.

"I will need Angus to keep watch," he decided.

He gave orders.

Chapter Thirty-Seven

Legacy

It was several weeks before Tearlach delivered the letter. Angus had returned and Ailean was irritable for several days thereafter. Tearlach watched as Ailean prowled Tarbert like a caged beast looking for a way out of his pen.

Tarbert was cool in summer in the mornings. The ocean breeze kept the outdoor temperature moderate except for occasional humid days when the air was still. Then, those that did not have to work outside, retreated behind the walls and let the stone shelter and cool them from the day's heat. They would emerge later when the sun was well past midday and take advantage of the ocean's cooling effect. When the sun dropped the stones would give off their heat keeping its residents warm until the early morning hours when the cycle would repeat.

Tearlach was unsure of what to do for his friend. He knew instinctively that the letter would not help. Not yet. Angus was spending a lot of time with the men. Tearlach noticed that he also looked unhappy. But Tearlach wasn't sure if it was due to some difference with Ailean or something to do with the men.

There were a number of new men in the castle. It made Tearlach uncomfortable. Over the years, men he knew had been lost. New men replaced them. They were all hard and distant. Tearlach felt he would not have the years it would take to know these newer men. Consequently, he always walked with his axe, even in the halls of Tarbert. His stride up and down the hallways was a fixture of the castle. Tearlach was always a restless individual; more at home in the forests and at sea than in the confines of a castle. His current clothing chafed, and the new leather boots were rubbing his heels raw. He wasn't in the best of moods he decided.

Raids had diminished in the past few

years. Ailean had spent more time than in the past with maintaining and running his lands. Tearlach noticed a slight limp in Ailean's gait when he first rose in the morning. Tearlach was sure that the people along the Northern Coast of Ireland were grateful for the reprieve, but Tearlach suspected that Ailean's men were growing restive.

It was about three weeks after Angus's return when Tearlach decided that it was time to deliver the letter.

Tearlach had carried if for the past four days looking for the right time. He found Ailean sitting in his favorite chair brooding.

He looked up when Tearlach came in and smiled wanly.

"So, what fine words do you have to cheer me today?"

Tearlach plunged in.

"I have a letter for you."

"A letter? From whom?"

"It is from Anne. She asked me to give it to you..."

He did a rapid calculation...

"in seven weeks after she left."

Ailean smiled.

"She always liked the number seven. Felt it was lucky. I wonder how her God feels about that?"

Tearlach breathed a silent sigh of relief.

"What does this letter say?"

"I have no idea. She sealed it and addressed it to you..."

"I see. Well you better let me have it. I'm sure she wants something."

His laugh was short, almost a bark. She always wanted something.

He opened the letter while Tearlach waited. He read silently for several minutes. Then he laughed loudly.

"She says, she wants me to change my ways. She says God wants me to repent."

He shook his head.

"God will have to send me a more direct message if he wants that."

He slapped the table.

"I'm doing well just as I am. Why would I want to change?"

He shook his head.

"Is that all?" said Tearlach.

"Of course not. The woman writes almost as much as she used to talk!"

Ailean looked down at the letter.

"She says that she has given me two fine sons and a daughter as a legacy - if only I wish to acknowledge them..."

Tearlach said nothing, but he could feel a small squeeze in his chest.

"If things had been different those children might have been mine..." he thought.

"She does have a point," said Ailean.

Tearlach looked up in surprise. Ailean's eyes seemed to be studying a tree on a painting across the room. His face looked wistful.

"I have lands and men in plenty. I also have two healthy sons and a daughter. It's time to get them ready to manage my estates."

Ailean was clearly lost in thought as spoke out loud. Fortunately, only Tearlach was there to hear.

"I could acknowledge the boys, make them legitimate, and put them in charge of Mingarry and Torloisk. It would certainly make my life easier. And who could I marry that daughter off to?"

Tearlach coughed.

"She's still a bit young for that."

"Nonsense," said Ailean. "I'm sure I could get a good alliance for her. She has her mother's eyes and features."

Then he shifted in his chair.

"But that can wait. There will be time enough for marriages. But there is one thing I can do now..."

* * *

Tearlach wrote the letter and sent it out with a ship which had a stop in Iona. The message was brief.

"I do not know if it was your plan and intent, or God's Will, but Ailean has acknowledged your sons and named them as his heirs..."

He thought about mentioning the marriage plans but decided it would be useless to speak of it.

Anne loved her daughter dearly. However, she could do nothing to protect the child, save accept her into the convent. Her recent and not too surprising elevation to Prioress assured that. Whatever Ailean decided would happen.

But, for the moment, Ailean had turned his attention to other matters. His men were getting restless with the long winter and little to do. Angus had mentioned this in a quiet meeting with Ailean a few days ago.

Summer was ending and soon the leaves would begin to turn. Tearlach wondered what the change in weather would bring.

Chapter Thirty-Eight

Foray for a Rib

Winter was almost over and the beef from the earlier raid was dwindling. Angus had been sitting with the younger men gauging their feelings. There had been several days of storms, not unusual for this time of year, but the weather had been on a cycle of storms that kept men indoors until tempers were stretched.

So, Tearlach was surprised when he heard Angus complain loud enough for all to hear.

"What a change has come over this house when the bones are so bare!"

He pointed at a rib from a scrawny calf they had slaughtered that morning.

A few men near him nodded.

Tearlach felt his face redden. To speak in Ailean's house in that way! If his axe were in hand, friend or not, he would have split Angus's skull.

He felt a gentle pull on his arm.

Next to him, Ailean raised a mug of ale. His face hidden, he whispered behind it.

"Take no offense! It is a signal we arranged," said Ailean.

"A signal? A signal for what?" thought Tearlach.

Ailean slammed the cup down so hard it shattered and stood.

"This meal is over!"

Men stopped eating and looked at him in surprise.

Ailean laughed loudly. It echoed through the hall.

"I am restless!" he shouted. "I want every birlinn ready to sail this evening!"

He pointed at the bones of the calf on the platter in front of him.

"Let's try to get a little more beef for the winter, shall we?"

Angus roared in approval. Others joined in.

Another cask of ale was rolled out and men drank and cheered and ran to make their boats and weapons ready.

Tearlach looked at Angus, who was now quietly talking with Ailean and understood.

Ailean had planned a foray and waited until Angus gave him the signal that the men were restless and getting ready to revolt. Then in one swift move he turned all their energy into a raid.

Tearlach sat back in admiration for the timing of the move. Then he rose to gather his weapons and shield.

Ailean would wait for no man this night and he wanted to be ready.

* * *

Ailean was smiling.

What a grand trip it had been!

His men had expected him to take them south, to assail some small Irish village. Initially they headed southeast as expected, down along the Kintyre peninsula, but instead of turning to sail southwest near the Earl of Argyll's Campbell stronghold at Skipness Castle he continued to sail southeast. His entire fleet sailed across to the Isle of Bute and then turned north, sheltering briefly in Glencallum Bay and taking on some water.

Leaving the bay, the fleet turned to the northeast sailing up the river Clyde to the dismay of those on the shore.

Ailean was in high spirits. He handed the tiller to Tearlach and made his way to the prow of the ship. He removed his helm and did a deep courtly bow as his ship passed Dumbarton Castle.

"Your pardon, Majesty, for the plunder we are about to take on your lands!

He stroked his beard and looked contrite. Then his head snapped up, he straightened, and he shouted.

"But my men are hungry for beef!"

He donned his helm to a round of laughter and came back to take the tiller from Tearlach.

He passed a lovely site, where the river forks with a large bay. Looking to the south saw a large herd of cattle grazing in a field, pointed, and led his boats ashore.

He laughed as his men spread out and gathered cattle while farmers ran and tried to hide their wives and daughters.

Tearlach stood next to him and smiled.

His luck had obviously returned. There had been no opposition to his raid, no one had expected his whole fleet to strike so far inland.

Resistance was just beginning to gather, and organized men were coming from the north, but his ships were nearly loaded.

He was reveling in his success, when Angus returned.

"The ships are ready to..."

The arrow was fired from so far away was nearly spent. But it caught Angus cleanly in the throat slicing through his neck behind the Adam's apple. Both jugular veins were caught by the arrow and began to bleed into his throat. He tried to cough but the blood choked him. He reached up and grabbed at the arrow which now stuck out both sides of his neck. His hands grabbed both ends and for a moment seemed confused as to which way to pull it out. Then his eyes rolled up in his head and he fell.

Tearlach caught him and rolled him on his back as he slumped.

He swiftly broke the arrow near the fletching and pulled it out. Blood spurted from both sides of his throat. The pain of removal brought Angus back to consciousness and he tried to speak, to breathe, and failed. His eyes grew larger as his struggles increased. His body began to quiver and shake.

Tearlach reached behind him to get his axe to end his friend's pain. But his axe was on the ground too far away to reach. He looked up to Ailean...

Ailean stood motionless, staring down the front of his coat covered in blood.

"Give me your axe," said Tearlach.

Ailean was slow in responding, looking out at the field instead.

By the time he reached out to hand the axe to Tearlach it was too late, Angus's eyes were locked wide in death. The blood pouring from the twin holes in his neck slowed and then stopped. Blood pooled in his mouth. Tearlach swiftly closed the eyes and tilted the head to let the blood drain out.

Sounds of fighting could be heard as the farmer's, returning with reinforcements to defend their homes and land, began to clash with Ailean's men.

Tearlach signaled and two younger men came over.

He pointed to the still form of Angus.

"Put him in the birlinn."

"He's dead," said one. "We could use the space for another cow."

"Tearlach stood up slowly and picked up his axe."

"Put him in the boat now, or the cow

will occupy the space where you used to sit."

The younger man looked at him belligerently for a moment and Tearlach was about to strike, when Ailean spoke.

"Tearlach, the lad's right. Load a cow. There's nothing we can do for him."

Tearlach whirled.

"He was your friend!"

"And now he's a corpse," said Ailean.

Tearlach's mouth opened but nothing came out.

Ailean looked to the two men and gestured to the field.

"Get another cow."

The two ran off.

Ailean turned back to Tearlach. His face was an impassive mask.

"You never show weakness, Tearlach. Never."

The eyes were cold but there was a hint of sadness there.

Tearlach nodded, knelt, and began stripping the body.

Ailean turned back to watch the slow withdrawal of his men.

Chapter Thirty-Nine

A Change of Heart

Tearlach and Ailean were alone on one of the conical tower battlements of Tarbert. The stone walls were damp with the morning air. A breeze had been blowing steadily all morning. Below them people were moving out into the fields for the day's labor. Behind him, he could hear the shouts of workmen. He could not make out the words and realized, once again, that his hearing was beginning to fail him. In the old days he could have heard every word of a conversation. Now, it was all just a muddle of voices.

Tales of the "foray for a rib" were spreading throughout the countryside. No one remembered it was Angus who said it.

Ailean rubbed his forehead. He put his hands on the stone of the battlement and not looking at Tearlach spoke out to the sea.

"Angus had been watching the men, especially the younger ones from Ireland and Wales for signs of rebellion. We had worked out a signal long ago to indicate when a revolt was close to happening. He used it that night."

"And the raid?" said Tearlach.

"I had been planning one for some time. I kept it in reserve for the right moment."

He sighed.

"Angus put most of the leaders of the revolt into the first ship that we landed. They were in the front line when the counter-attack came. We didn't take many losses, but those that fell were mostly the leaders."

He smiled.

"It was actually Angus's idea. Best one he ever had. 'Give 'em what they really want,' he said."

His voice was bitter.

"And we did."

He looked down.

The arrow you took from Angus's

throat. Did you notice it?

Tearlach shook his head.

"It was Welsh. One of ours. A new lad. I recognized the fletching. It was meant for me. He was on the first boat that landed and never got back on the boat when we left. I was looking for him. He must've died in the raid."

His hands clenched the stone wall, fingers digging into unyielding rock. He looked down at the damp stone.

"I can't avenge Angus."

He straightened slightly and looked up and out across the water.

"I thought I had my old luck back."

His laugh was even more bitter.

"Once, I mocked God when talking to Anne, and asked for a sign. Well, I got one."

He coughed twice, surprising Tearlach.

"I'm getting old, and I'm tired, Tearlach."

Ailean slapped the stone with an open palm.

"Angus had identified the ringleaders and those who will follow them. In the spring I will arrange for those who remain to be grouped into two ships to do a foray. The two leaders who are most hostile to each other will lead with their men in each of the boats. We'll include most the Irish and Welshmen as well. Then I'll send them to the Irish Coast.

The sea, the Irish, and their own tempers will settle the rest."

Tearlach stood quietly thinking. The number of men was already reduced by the foray and would be further reduced by the loss of two full crews.

He had no doubt that those on the foray would not return.

Ailean would be left with older men who were veterans and accustomed to following orders from Ailean. He would have peace for a few years if he kept the men busy. Several were already looking at growing families that would take a lot of energy to handle.

Ailean sighed heavily.

"My brother will be disappointed. I'm sure that he will miss the spy reports he was getting from Angus…"

Tearlach's mouth opened but nothing came out.

Ailean smiled at his confusion. And began answering questions before Tearlach could ask.

"How long has Angus been a spy for my brother? Since the beginning. At first, I was sure he would try and plant a couple of spies, perhaps an assassin. He knew I was leaving from the beginning. He'd been trying to drive me out even before he found out about my 'inheritance'. That just accelerated the process. He was behind the spread of what happened at Cairnburg, of course.

He took another sip of ale.

"But Angus was just a bit too good. He was exactly what I was looking for. I was suspicious from the beginning. I'm not sure if he was supposed to kill me in that first confrontation or simply back down, but I suspect the former."

He sighed again.

"Family politics is such a messy thing. I was too close in age and he saw me as a threat to his becoming Laird when my father died. He sent me the forged letter from Mary, of course, though at the time I didn't know. Later I wondered if it was a prank gone wrong or deliberately malicious to ruin me in the eyes of father. Later it became a lever to keep us apart. I think mother suspected the truth."

"By making Angus a captain I put him in a place where he could see what I wanted him to see. My brother sent other spies, of course, but there was no point in trying for a higher position in my organization. They would simply serve as messengers to my brother. No other could gather as much information as he could."

Ailean took a small drink.

"I was sure I was correct when he returned with the extra birlinn. It was far too easy to steal. And I'm sure my brother told Angus to ally himself with Anne to get Hector of Coll freed."

Tearlach finally managed to get his voice working.

"Why?"

"Holding a MacLean in my dungeon without him taking any action was putting too great a strain on his rule over the other MacLeans. If I didn't set him free soon, he would have to come and free him or kill me to maintain his authority."

He chuckled.

"Angus must have been most nervous when he reported that the king had taken Eachann hostage. He had lost his support at Duart, and in reporting it to me he may have suspected that I would finally realize that he was a spy. How else could he have gotten the information so quickly? Eachann sent someone to tell him before he was taken."

"I think that by that time Eachann

had figured out I never wanted to be Laird of Duart. It's too restrictive. I found the thing I was destined for. As a pirate captain I have gained all I ever wanted... until now."

Ailean looked out at a birlinn sailing out of the harbor and pointed it out to Tearlach. It was Ailean's. It raised sail and the Crest of MacLean billowed out in the breeze. The ship leaped forward.

"That ship carries word to Anne. She has been sending me letters for almost a year now, asking me to change my ways."

He smiled.

"Damned woman always got her way with me in the end. I should have known this time would be no different."

He looked from the ship back to the sky.

"The adventure is over, Tearlach. I'm leaving the sea. It's time to make my peace with God if I can."

Chapter Forty

Reforming

Anne was surprised by the letter she received from Ailean. She walked the convent grounds at Iona and read the letter again. It wasn't humble - begging God for forgiveness. That was not his style. But it did acknowledge that he was going to change, and Anne knew that Ailean was a man of his word. That gave her comfort.

The sun was warm as she walked and there was a fresh breeze in the air. She felt a sudden chill and wished she had brought something to put around her to fend off the cold.

He sent gifts of money, which was also like him.

"He thinks he can buy his way to heaven," she thought.

The reaction of the monks had been uncharacteristically generous.

They offered up prayers for him and joined her and the sisters in asking for God to grant him a chance at redemption.

She hoped he would eventually understand that money could not be used to buy your way into the kingdom of heaven.

She hoped he would have enough time to discover that.

She would have to write him back, immediately.

"His chance at redemption is slight, surrounded by so much violence and political intrigue. Any delay from me, might cost him his chance at paradise."

Her letter to him expressed her joy at his search and a careful Biblical warning about a rich man, a camel, and the eye of a needle.

She was sure he would get the message.

* * *

Perhaps Ailean did, but the largesse from Tarbert continued to come. Over the course of several months, men came to work on the church and chapel. Food for the winter came, enough to feed the monks, the sisters, and the workmen. There was even enough for the poor of the island.

As the years passed, she walked the newly tended grounds and marveled at the change that had come over the brothers and sisters in her order. They seemed more animated and livelier. While they maintained solemnity during services, she could see an increased gaiety in their regular lives.

She stood looking out over the ocean from her favorite spot in the early evening. It was the perfect place to rest. The sky was cloudless and the blue seemed to reach from horizon to horizon growing deeper as she looked to the east.

"He was always right when we disagreed about how people would behave," she thought. *"Why should now be any different?"*

* * *

Her final surprise was a late arriving letter that came in the autumn. In it, Ailean spoke of helping a farmer in the fields at Tarbert. He enjoyed the peace of working with the earth and had started tending a small garden.

She too had started a small garden here on Iona. It was mostly vegetables and herbs which she shared with the sisters and brothers. However, a small piece was set aside with the flowers she loved from Treshnish. Several were late in blossoming and had given her comfort when she felt the chill in her bones.

That night she blessed herself before bed and thanked God for Ailean's transformation and gave Him praise for the changes He had wrought in such a violent man.

The next day she saw a sleek birlinn she recognized. The sail carried the crest of the MacLeans. The borders of the sail were black. At the top of the mast flew a black flag. Before it even landed, she knelt sadly and offered up a different kind of prayer.

A prayer for the reposed of the soul.

Chapter Forty-One

Passing

Ailean lay quietly in his bed. The day's work had been hard. His chest and arms were aching, and he was sweating even after he finished and poured cold water over himself.

He didn't have a very good appetite, though he and Tearlach joked as usual. Tearlach had remarked loudly that he had made 19 forays. Ailean had replied that if he had known he would have made it an even score. This brought laughter from around the table. But his favorite ale tasted sour tonight and he felt tired. He was dizzy with relief to finally slip into bed. Tomorrow, he hoped the ache would be gone and he could finally get back to work. It was strange, but after all these years of looking down on them, he was finally beginning to see that maybe the farmers were right. There was some good in working the land.

* * *

His daughter ran to see, when a servant burst in with the news. She stopped at the doorway, stood quietly for a moment, then blessed herself. The servants stood behind her frozen in the hallway.

Her father lay still in his bed. His chest did not move. His eyes were open. She smiled. His face was completely at peace. She tiptoed forward and gently closed the eyelids.

Then she left and closed the door.

"Tearlach should know," she thought.

* * *

Tearlach looked down at the still form of his friend. His eyes fought tears. He blinked, turned to servants and forced himself to speak.

"Prepare his best clothes and summon his sons from their homes. We will dress him."

As they moved to obey, he added.

"And bring his axe and shield."

He looked back to the still face of his companion.

"He would want them."

* * *

When Eachann heard the news, he ordered all his men to leave him. He walked the empty hallways where he and his brother had plotted the downfall of men, castles, and clans.

He walked over to a small cupboard and poured from a small keg of ale. It was a favorite of Ailean's. Eachann hated it. They always drank it together. Now Eachann raised his glass one more time.

His thoughts wandered over their lives.

"You were a great puzzle to me at times brother, so loyal and yet so cruel. We played many games, both together and against each other."

He took a deep swallow. The ale was bitter. And, for just a moment, he thought he understood why Ailean liked it.

"But now, the games are finally over. Now you play one more time with God."

264

He paused then spoke aloud.

"This time, I hope you win."

He drained the glass, smashed the cup in the fireplace and walked out onto the battlements of Duart castle to reminisce.

* * *

Anne received word a few days later. Tearlach sent a ship with a black flag tied to the mast, to Iona with a letter addressed to Anne. She didn't need to read it - the sail was enough - but the way he had passed cheered her and convinced her that he had been forgiven.

She prayed at the MacLean Cross and then went to the chapel and prayed for the rest of the day, saying rosary after rosary, working through the entire set of stations of the cross. When she was finally done, she asked

Photo 7 - The MacLean Cross on Iona

265

to see the head monk.

She petitioned and was granted permission for his burial at Iona. He had spent a great deal of money on Iona, and the monks came to appreciate her argument that he may have actually repented. It was not an easy case to plead, but she had sway and she used every bit to get him a place on the Isle.

Here, she argued, she could watch over him, pray for him, and hopefully bring him some peace. He was surely a troubled soul.

Of this, no monk could disagree.

Chapter Forty-Two

Last Voyage

Standing quietly while the grave was being slowly filled, Tearlach looked at those who gathered around.

Eachann was not present, for which Tearlach was oddly grateful. Ailean's sons, Hector and John were present, as was his daughter. She hung in the background silent and oddly beautiful.

Anne was there, of course, with the other nuns as Prioress. They prayed and they sang for the soul of Ailean MacLean.

Tearlach was surprised at how lovely Anne's voice was. He had never heard her sing.

At the conclusion of the service they

each dropped a handful of dirt in the grave. His daughter added a flower, but Tearlach did not know what kind it was.

The nuns each came and offered a short blessing. Anne was last. Her head bent for a moment as her lips moved in silent prayer. Then she bent and tossed a last handful of dirt in the grave. With it went a small rosary from around her neck.

Men moved in to fill the grave and the family moved away. The children hugged their mother who blessed them in turn, oldest to youngest, and they departed.

He stood quietly watching while the grave was filled in, feeling part of his life closing with each spade full of dirt.

He was surprised that Anne stayed as

Photo 8 - Nan Sop's burial cover on Iona

well. When the job was done, she gave each of the men a small coin and a blessing and they left as well.

They were all that remained.

She smiled and came over to him.

"I knew you would be here Tearlach," she said.

"Others would have come, but a fleet of pirate ships descending on Iona would probably be misinterpreted," he said dryly.

She laughed and they stood quietly for a moment.

"It is a beautiful spot," he said.

There was a smile on her face as she looked around.

"Yes, it's my favorite spot."

Tearlach nodded and finally made himself speak though he wasn't sure if it would offer any consolation.

"I think he was hurt when you left. But I also think he understood. It was tough for him to lose another person he loved. He loved so few."

She smiled.

"Oh, I think he cared for me, but he was only in love with his memory of Mary MacNeil."

"His memory?"

"Yes," she said. "He had a vision of how they were kids playing at love, rebuffing each other but secretly still wanting each other. That didn't change even after he went over that cliff."

"Well," said Tearlach, "He's gone, and I think he's finally at peace."

"Yes, I believe he finally got his real wish," said Anne. "He has been buried on holy ground here in Iona with the knowledge that someone cares about him more than anyone else."

"You?" said Tearlach.

"No," she said. "God."

Tearlach shrugged. He wasn't sure that it was really his real desire. Just as he wasn't sure that, in the end, Ailean didn't come to love Anne - as well as his memory of Mary MacNeil.

Tearlach smiled. The air was fresh from a strong sea breeze. And Tearlach felt it was also time for him to clear the air.

"I was always in love with you," he said.

Anne smiled slowly.

She took both his hands and squeezed them gently.

"Oh Tearlach, I always knew you were interested in me, even when we were young. A girl can tell. I was just glad that you never pursued it."

"Why?" he asked stung.

Her smile fell a bit.

"Because my answer would have been, 'No.'"

She looked into his eyes. He was surprised that they were misting slightly

"Tearlach, a woman knows how much she is loved. It can take time to see how much, but in the end, she can sense it."

Her voice was flat.

"When we agreed to handfast, Ailean did not love me."

"But, I did!" he blurted.

"Yes, you did."

There was a gentleness as she released his hands and looked to the grave.

"But, never as much as you loved Ailean..."

Acknowledgments

Normally acknowledgments are at the front of the book, but they are in the back for electronic titles so that the system can present more of the books opening if something like Kindle is used which automatically generates 10% of the books content as an incentive.

A lot of work went into the creation of this book. And while the story (and the mistakes) are all mine. I want to acknowledge those who try to keep me from making a complete fool of myself - in content, consistency, and grammatically.
So, thank you to my content editor, my grammar checker, my spelling checker, and the people who keep me in coffee and good cheer while I create these stories.

I hope you enjoyed the story. If you did then a favorable review would go a long way towards directing others to this book. If would like to share your opinion you can submit reviews to Goodreads, Amazon and to Barnes and Noble. I've enclosed starting links for you below.

To reach Goodreads try...
http://www.goodreads.com

To reach Amazon try...
http://www.amazon.com/books

To reach Barnes and Noble try...
http://www.barnesandnoble.com/b/books

For Nook Books try
http://www.barnesandnoble.com/b/nook_boo
ks

About the Author

David Nash is an award-winning author of works spanning from science fiction, to steam-punk, to fantasy, to mysteries. He has several books to his credit including *Hayden's War, Ben's War, Ashes and Ruin, Scythe of Cronos*, and has written short stories included in such works as *Tales of Isgalduin.* This is his first foray into historical fiction.

Printed in Poland
by Amazon Fulfillment
Poland Sp. z o.o., Wrocław